"Is Kate here?" asked Cooper, pulling off her second boot in the doorway of Crones' Circle and coming to stand by Annie.

"She's in the back," Annie said. "She's helping set up."

Cooper nodded. "Remind you of anything?" she asked Annie as they watched the snow.

"You mean Yule?" replied Annie. "I was just thinking that. But this is no magic snowstorm. This is just Mother Nature giving one final blowout before spring comes along."

"Yes," Cooper said, "but how convenient that it just happened to come along on the night of our big test."

"Speaking of which," Annie said, "they're all being *way* mysterious about that."

"Big shock," said Cooper. "Witches being mysterious. I'm surprised they aren't blindfolding us like they did at our dedication ceremony."

"There's still time," Annie remarked, laughing.

Follow the Circle:

circle of three

book
14

the challenge box

isobel bird

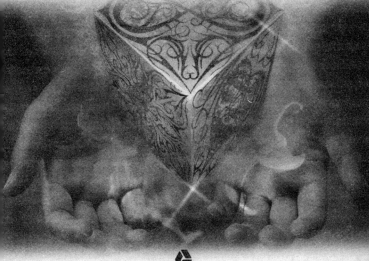

AVON BOOKS

An Imprint of HarperCollinsPublishers

Library of Congress Catalog Card Number: 2001118054
ISBN 0-06-000606-4

First Avon edition, 2002

❖

AVON TRADEMARK REG. U.S. PAT. OFF. AND IN OTHER COUNTRIES,
MARCA REGISTRADA, HECHO EN U.S.A.

Visit us on the World Wide Web!
www.harperteen.com

circle of three

the challenge box

CHAPTER 1

Cooper pushed open the door of Crones' Circle, stepped inside, and shut the door behind her. "That is a *lot* of snow," she remarked as she removed the black knit hat she was wearing and shook off the stubborn white flakes that clung to her dark blue wool jacket. She ran her hands through her hair, which was suffering from having been confined beneath the hat, and wiped her boots on the mat that Archer had placed near the door to prevent people from tracking snow and dirt across the store's wood floor. A line of shoes and boots sat beside it, a further hint that the proprietors would prefer their customers to go shoeless.

"Is it still coming down hard?" asked Annie, who was perusing the latest additions to the store's stock of books. She had removed her own boots and was walking around in her socks.

"I took the bus instead of driving," Cooper told her, bending down to take off her boots and add them to those already lined up by the door. "You can hardly see out there."

Annie went to the window and peered out. In the light of the street lamps she could see snowflakes swirling madly, like moths fluttering around a candle flame. On the street outside the shop the snow blanketed the sidewalks, and the fire hydrant on the corner looked like a tiny snowman. *More like a snow gnome*, Annie thought happily, enjoying the way the snow made everything look enchanted.

"Is Kate here?" asked Cooper, pulling off her second boot and coming to stand by Annie.

"She's in the back," Annie said. "She's helping set up."

Cooper nodded. "Remind you of anything?" she asked Annie as they watched the snow.

"You mean Yule?" replied Annie. "I was just thinking that. But this is no magic snowstorm," she added, referring to the blizzard that had threatened to turn their week at a remote hotel, where they had gone to celebrate the Winter Solstice two months before, into a long winter's nap of the permanent variety. "This is just Mother Nature giving one final blowout before spring comes along."

"Yes," Cooper said, "but how convenient that it just happened to come along on the night of our big test."

"Speaking of which," Annie said, "they're all being *way* mysterious about that."

"Big shock," said Cooper. "Witches being

mysterious. I'm surprised they aren't blindfolding us like they did at our dedication ceremony."

"There's still time," Annie remarked, laughing.

"Did you get *anything* out of them?" Cooper asked her as they turned and walked toward the rear of the store and the room where they held their weekly Wicca study group.

Annie shook her head. "Not really," she replied. "All Sophia would say was that we were going to be facing a final challenge. Then she disappeared into the back office and hasn't come out."

"She's probably afraid we'll use cunning and guile to make her talk," said Cooper jokingly. "Or just nag her until she can't stand it anymore."

They walked into the meeting room, where they found Kate arranging cushions on the floor. "Oh, sure," she said sternly as she saw her friends, "come in when all the *hard* work is done."

"Hey," Cooper said, pretending to be offended, "I was out there shoveling a path to the front door."

Kate laughed. "All right," she said. Then she pointed an accusing finger at Annie. "But *you* were definitely skipping out on me."

"But you arrange cushions so well," said Annie.

Kate snorted. "Flattery will get you nowhere," she said, sitting down. "I'm immune to your charms."

Annie and Cooper joined her on the floor. It felt good to be inside, where it was warm, while outside the snow fell, wrapping the world in cold. As usual, there was incense burning on the little altar in the store, and the air was scented with the rich smells of cedar and sage. In the meeting space, candles placed around the room gave off cheerful light, and soft music played on the store's CD player, something harplike and dreamy.

"Can you believe this weather?" asked Kate as they relaxed and waited for the other members of the class to arrive.

"We were talking about that before we came in," said Cooper. "It's very omenlike."

"I wasn't even thinking about that," Kate responded. "I was just thinking about how cold it is."

"Well, we only have to put up with it for three more days," Annie said. "I can guarantee you that there will be no snow in New Orleans. I talked to Juliet before I came over here, and she said it's eighty-two degrees there today."

"How do you feel about seeing your big sister for the first time?" Cooper asked her, referring to the fact that they were going to New Orleans so that Annie could meet the sister that, until recently, she hadn't even known she had.

Annie looked thoughtful. "Excited," she said. "And scared," she added after a moment. "I'm glad you guys are going with me."

Kate sighed. "I can't wait to get there," she said. "I am *so* stoked about this trip. Thank Goddess my mom has that wedding to cater. She's so distracted with planning it that I don't think she quite realizes that she's letting me go during Mardi Gras."

"My mother knows, all right," Cooper said. "If she reminds me one more time to be careful I think I'm going to start drinking."

Annie and Kate looked at her, shocked. "I can't believe you said that," exclaimed Kate.

Cooper rolled her eyes. "Please," she said. "We are so beyond the days of the after-school special. This isn't some deep dark secret we aren't supposed to talk about. My mother had a little drinking problem. Now she's dealing. I'm not going to pretend it didn't happen."

"So everything is okay?" asked Kate hesitantly.

Cooper shrugged. "More or less," she said. "She's still going to her group. She and T.J.'s mom have really hit it off. I think it freaks him out a little, like they're planning our wedding when they go out for dinner or something." She paused for a moment, then looked at her friends with a horrified expression on her face. "You don't think they are, do you?" she asked.

"Most definitely," said Kate, looking at Annie. "I bet they've even picked out your dress."

"And I bet it's *totally* frilly," Annie said.

The three of them cracked up, and they were still laughing when Archer walked into the room. She was carrying something in her arms. It looked like a box, but because it was covered with a black cloth they couldn't tell exactly what it was. Archer set it down on a table, then turned to the girls.

"I'm going to go back in there to help Sophia," she

said. "I don't want *any* peeking under here. Got it?"

Cooper, Kate, and Annie stared at the mysterious item. They all nodded.

"Good," Archer said. "And don't even think about cheating. I'll *know*."

She disappeared, leaving the girls to sit looking at the thing on the table.

"What do you think it is?" Annie asked after a moment.

"I'm going to go peek," said Cooper, starting to get up.

"No!" Kate and Annie said in unison, pulling Cooper back down.

Cooper groaned, but she sat down and didn't try to get up again. They continued to look at the mystery shape as, one by one, their classmates came into the room and took their seats. Everybody wanted to know what the thing beneath the cloth was, and the room buzzed with their conversations. Then Sophia and Archer appeared from the back room, and everyone stopped talking and looked at them.

"Well," Sophia said, her eyes sparkling, "I bet I can guess what you all want to know." She paused and looked at their expectant faces, not saying anything else.

"What is it?" Cooper blurted out, unable to contain herself any longer.

"That is your final challenge," Sophia informed the students. "Well, let me clarify—it *contains* your final challenge."

She walked over to the table and pulled the black cloth away. Beneath it was a box. But it wasn't just any box. This box was painted on all sides with beautiful designs. Intricate Celtic knotwork twisted around the top edge, and the center panel of each side was decorated with a different magical symbol. Sophia let everyone get a good look at the box before continuing.

"A little more than ten months ago, you each underwent a dedication ceremony," she said. "At that ceremony each one of you selected a word of power from the cauldron. Those words were meant to inspire you on your journey during this past year. They were also meant as challenges. In all likelihood, the words you chose have popped up again and again in different forms, am I right?"

All around the room heads nodded in agreement. Kate, Annie, and Cooper were most definitely in agreement with Sophia's statement. The words they had chosen at that ritual—*healing* for Annie, *connection* for Cooper, and *truth* for Kate— had been recurring themes in the many different obstacles they'd each faced while studying witchcraft. In their own ways, each one of the girls had come to understand her chosen word and the importance of it in her life and in her journey.

"Just as you chose your words of power to begin your journey, you're now going to choose another challenge to end it," Sophia told them. She indicated the box. "This is the Challenge Box," she said.

"Inside are a number of slips of paper. Each one has a challenge written on it. Each of you will select a challenge. Whatever you select will be the final test you will undergo before it is decided whether or not you're ready for full initiation as witches."

"Sort of like when Dorothy had to get the broomstick of the Wicked Witch of the West," remarked Cooper. "That doesn't sound too bad."

Sophia raised an eyebrow. "Really?" she said. "There are many past class members who would disagree with you about that," she added cryptically. "And Dorothy had her friends to help her. You'll each be on your own."

"What kind of challenges are they?" Annie asked.

"All kinds," answered Sophia. "Some ask you to perform a particular task. Others require you to find something out. Each challenge is unique to the person choosing it. Or should I say to the person it chooses."

"So if we pass the challenge, we're in?" Kate said.

"Not quite," Sophia answered. "The final challenge is only one of the things we consider when deciding whether or not a candidate is ready for initiation. However, I will say that if you fail to complete your challenge then it's very unlikely that you'll be asked to undergo initiation. But we have a way to go before we reach the point of making those decisions. Right now it's time to find out what your challenges are. Who wants to go first?"

"I do," Kate said, earning looks of surprise from her friends, as well as from Sophia and Archer. She blushed. "I know, I usually don't volunteer to go first. But I want to get it over with."

She stood up and walked to the box. At first she wasn't sure how she was supposed to get anything out of it, as there was no discernible lid and there didn't seem to be any way of opening it. For a moment she panicked, thinking that maybe *this* was the test and she was failing it. Then she noticed that the center of the box's top panel was actually a circle of black velvet, and not wood. She poked at it with her finger and discovered that there was a slit in the velvet. She pushed her hand through and into the box.

Just as Sophia had promised, the box was filled with slips of paper. Touching them with her fingers, Kate was reminded once more of the dedication ceremony and how she'd hesitated before selecting the slip of paper with her word on it. That time she'd been terrified about what accepting the challenge meant for her life. Now she was afraid again, but for a different reason. This time she knew what accepting the challenge meant, but part of her was terrified that she might not be able to meet it. Then what would happen? If she wasn't accepted for initiation, she would have gone through a lot of trouble for nothing.

She pushed her fears away, knowing that thinking about them wasn't going to help. One thing she'd learned about magic was that you had to meet it head-on. Before she could second-guess herself anymore, she grabbed a slip of paper and pulled it out. She looked at it, then looked at Sophia.

"Do I tell everyone what it is?" she asked.

"No," answered Sophia. "You should show me and Archer, because we need to know so that we can see how well you accomplish your challenge. Other than that, I recommend keeping your challenges to yourselves."

Kate looked at her paper again, then showed it to Sophia and Archer. Archer, who was holding a notebook, wrote down Kate's challenge. When she was done she nodded at Kate. "Good luck," she said.

Kate returned to her seat, the slip of paper clutched in her hand. She thought about what was written on her paper. Would she be able to do it? She hoped so. But she wasn't sure. She looked at Cooper and Annie, who were seated beside her, watching the proceedings. She very much wanted to discuss her challenge with her friends, to see what they made of the task she'd been assigned. But Sophia had told them not to. It was going to be up to her, and her alone, to figure out exactly what the words on her slip of paper meant. For the moment all she could do was watch as the others went forward to reach into the Challenge Box.

Annie was the second of the threesome to go forward. She reached in and felt around. She stirred the slips of paper with her hand, hoping that some feeling—some sign—would come to her when she touched the right one. But there were no flashes of light, no trumpet blasts or voices telling her to pick a particular slip.

You're overanalyzing this, she told herself. *That scientific brain of yours is working overtime. Just go with what you feel.*

She closed her eyes, stirred some more, grabbed a handful of slips, and then let all of them but one fall from her fingers. The one that remained behind she pulled out. She showed it to Archer and Sophia before she even looked at it herself. After she'd read it, she folded it carefully and tucked it into her pocket as she returned to her seat.

Cooper waited an unusually long time before standing up and walking to the Challenge Box. But unlike Kate and Annie, once she was standing in front of it she didn't hesitate at all. She plunged her hand in, snatched up the first slip she touched, and pulled it out. She read it, an indecipherable expression passing over her face as she did so, and then presented it to Sophia and Archer to be recorded in the book. Then she walked back to her friends and sat down.

The three friends sat and waited for the other class participants to finish choosing their challenges. None of them said anything to the others, but it was clear that they were all thinking about their own challenges. When the last person had drawn a slip from the box, Archer closed her notebook and

11

Sophia put the black cover over the Challenge Box once more.

"Now you have your challenges," Sophia said. "You have two weeks to complete them. We won't have class next week, and will meet again on the fourteenth of March. At that time you will each be expected to give a short description of your challenge and how you did—or did not—complete it."

"That's it?" asked Cooper, sounding surprised.

"You expected more?" asked Sophia, laughing.

"Well, yeah," Cooper said. "This is the last class, right?"

"The last regular class, yes," Sophia answered. "After class on the fourteenth, only those people preparing for initiation will meet. There will be four preparatory classes, with the initiation following on April the thirteenth."

"Right," Cooper said. "So this is really the last class. Shouldn't we *do* something?"

"Oh," Sophia said. "Now I see what you're getting at." She and Archer were grinning broadly, as if they had been keeping a secret from the class. "You mean like a party?"

"Yeah," Cooper said. "Like a party."

Sophia looked at Archer. "Think you can work some magic and get us a party?"

Archer nodded. "I think I can come up with a party spell," she said. She cleared her throat and looked solemnly at the class. "Party gods and goddesses," she said, "come to us and bring the fun. Send us music, send us munchies, now that all our work is done."

No sooner had she finished speaking than several people emerged from the back carrying trays of food and things to drink. They were members of the various covens involved in putting the class together, and when the class saw them they clapped and cheered.

"Party time!" called out one of the men carrying a plate of brownies. His long white hair and beard were tied with multicolored ribbons, and as he walked around the room handing brownies to people, he shook his hips like a hula dancer.

"Leave it to Thatcher," remarked Cooper to her friends as they watched their friend from the Coven of the Green Wood. Although he was one of the older members, he was always the first one to take part in any festivities.

The harp music that had been playing changed to something more lively as someone popped a new CD into the player, and the room immediately took on a party atmosphere as everybody began talking and eating. Annie, Cooper, and Kate stood together, chewing Thatcher's brownies and talking.

"I know we can't say exactly what our challenges are," Cooper said, her mouth full, "but what do you guys think of yours?"

Kate and Annie looked at each other. "I'm not sure I understand mine," Kate said.

"I understand mine," Annie said. "At least I understand what it says. But I don't know if I understand exactly how to do it."

Cooper nodded. "Same here," she said.

"You're not discussing your challenges, are you?" Archer said, sneaking up on them.

"Only in the most basic of ways," said Annie. "Promise you won't bust us?"

"Well, okay," Archer replied. "But enough serious stuff. Let's dance."

She took Annie by the hand and dragged her off to start a spiral dance. Soon many of the others had joined in, leaving their plates of food and cups of drink for later. Cooper and Kate were swept up in the dancing as well. As they celebrated the end of class with their friends and classmates, they laughed and sang. But in the back of each one's mind was the challenge she would soon face.

CHAPTER 2

There's no way, Kate thought grimly as she bit off a piece of carrot stick and chewed on it. *I just don't get it.* She was thinking about the challenge she'd picked the night before. At first, she'd been able to not overanalyze it too much. Yes, the words of the challenge were a little cryptic, but she'd told herself during the party that it would all come clear once she'd had a chance to sit and think it over.

Well, now she *had* had a chance to sit and think it over. She'd thought about it for most of the night, once she'd gotten home and into bed. And it hadn't helped. All she'd been able to do was go over the challenge again and again in her head, wondering what it might mean. She did it again now, seeing the words that were written on the slip of paper scroll across her thoughts: "Answer the question that has no answer."

How can a question have no answer? she asked herself. *If it's a question, then there's an answer to it. It* seemed pretty obvious to her. But clearly she was a moron, quite possibly the stupidest almost-witch there ever was. *I bet Sabrina or Willow would know the answer right off the top of their heads*, she thought dully.

"Hey there."

Kate looked up and saw Tara and Jessica. They sat down at the table and opened their lunch bags, taking out plastic containers and opening the lids.

"What's yours?" Tara asked Jessica.

"Pasta salad," replied Jessica. "And I *told* my mother that I'm doing the no-carbs thing."

"Mine's grilled chicken," said Tara.

The two girls swapped containers wordlessly and began eating from them. Jessica, stabbing a piece of chicken with her fork, turned to Kate. "So, you excited about New Orleans?"

"What?" asked Kate, still stewing over her challenge. "Oh, yeah, I am."

"You're going to *love* it," Tara told her. "I went once with my parents to some jazz festival. That part was dullsville, but the city is so cool. Anne Rice lives there, you know. Ooh, maybe you'll see her!"

"Maybe," said Kate. "But it's Mardi Gras, so there will probably be, like, sixty billion people there. I'm sure Anne will be in hiding."

"I hear she likes to walk around in costume during Mardi Gras," Jessica said knowingly. "You probably wouldn't be able to recognize her anyway."

Tara sighed. "I wish I was going, too," she said. "But no. I get to spend my break right here in thrilling

Beecher Falls, the world capital of excruciating boredom."

"Look on the bright side," Jessica replied. "You can get your English paper done."

"Oh, right," Tara said with mock excitement. "Because reading *Jane Eyre* is *so* much more fun than going to New Orleans."

Kate listened as her friends continued chatting, letting their voices fade into the background as she resumed thinking about her challenge. It just didn't make any sense to her. How could she answer a question if she didn't know what it was? And how could she answer it if it had no answer? *Why couldn't I get something easy, like slaying a dragon?* she thought miserably.

She wondered what challenges Cooper and Annie had drawn. On the bus ride home from class, they had talked about everything except the one thing they all really wanted to talk about. Kate had been surprised at how hard it was to keep her challenge a secret. After all, Annie and Cooper were her best friends. She was used to sharing practically everything with them, especially when it came to magical stuff. They'd started the class together, and they'd gone through a lot of difficult things together. But now that they were facing their final challenges, she wasn't allowed to ask for their help. It was frustrating having to do it all on her own. Was it as hard for her friends? She didn't know, but the insecure, worried part of her was pretty much convinced that while she was suffering, still just trying to *understand* her challenge, her friends had already completed theirs. She pictured them all at the initiation ceremony, Cooper and Annie smiling triumphantly as Sophia and the others did whatever they did to make them real witches, while she stood in the back watching, having failed her test. It was too much to even consider.

And thinking of failing just reminded her that she was now officially failing Ms. Ableman's science class. After having the unfortunate luck of being paired with her arch nemesis, Sherrie, for a big-deal lab project that counted for a huge chunk of their grade, Kate had ruined any chance of getting by when she had let Sherrie's incompetence get to her and had started a catfight with her rival. Their experiment had been completely ruined, Ms. Ableman hadn't budged even after Kate had apologized, and the end result was that Kate was facing a big F in that class. Even the joy she'd experienced from dumping several pots of dirt on Sherrie's head couldn't make up for the fact that for the first time in her life, Kate was probably going to be forced to take a class over again.

She hadn't been able to tell her parents about the F. Report cards for the period hadn't been sent home yet, and she hoped Mr. and Mrs. Morgan wouldn't find out about the disaster until she was back from New Orleans. If they'd known about it, they would never have agreed to let her go. Kate was sure of that. She felt a little guilty about hiding her failing mark from them, but she tried not to think about that. *After all*, she thought, resorting to the justification she'd been using to make herself feel better about not being entirely forthcoming with her parents, *Sherrie started it*.

"And gumbo," Tara said, jarring Kate out of her thoughts. "You have got to try gumbo. I wish you could bring us back some."

"Right," Kate said. She hadn't heard anything her friends had been saying, but they didn't seem to notice. "Gumbo."

For the rest of lunch she faded in and out of the conversation, sometimes listening to what Jessica and Tara were talking about but more often than not thinking about her own problems. When the bell signaling the next period rang, she got up with a sense of relief and tossed her garbage into the trash before leaving. She loved her friends, but she was so preoccupied with her own thoughts at the moment that she wanted to be alone.

Sadly, her next class was algebra. Math had never been one of her favorite subjects, and the fact that she had Ms. Ableman's science class right afterward made it even less appealing. While Mr. Niemark rambled on about cosines and factors and other things Kate couldn't possibly care less about, she found herself writing in her notebook. But she wasn't taking notes on the lecture. She was making a list. Maybe, she thought, if she could come up with some ideas, she could get started on her challenge. At the top of a clean page she wrote:

Questions that Possibly Have No Answers
1. What is the meaning of life?
2. Why did the chicken cross the road?
3. If a tree falls and no one hears it, does it make a sound?
4. Is the glass half full or half empty?

She looked at her list and then added:
5. Could I be a bigger idiot?

The list was not helping. While perhaps the questions she was coming up with *were* valid ones (although she couldn't possibly imagine why), she knew they weren't what the challenge was about. That would be stupid. No, her question had to have something to do with witchcraft. That was the only thing that made sense. But what? Was there some ancient question that witches had been trying to find the answer to for centuries? Was there some legend that centered around an unanswerable question? Maybe it was a trick. Maybe she was being challenged on her knowledge of Wiccan lore.

That cheered her up a little. Maybe Sophia and the others were just trying to fool her into thinking the challenge was harder than it really was. Maybe all she had to do was figure out what story they were referring to. Perhaps her challenge was like the kind the people in fairy tales were always being presented with, like finding the key to a glass mountain, or locating a castle that lay east of the sun and west of the moon. *That has to be it*, she thought, feeling very clever for having figured out at least part of the challenge. Now she just had to find out what this mysterious question was. Fairy tales and legends had never been her strong suit, but how hard could it be to do some reading? She'd go to the library during ninth period, when she had study hall.

Feeling a lot more optimistic than she'd felt since selecting her slip of paper from the Challenge Box, Kate turned her attention back to Mr. Niemark and algebra. She still didn't have much interest in the subject, but at least she was able to concentrate a little more fully now that she'd taken the first step on the road to completing her mission. As she'd been reminded over and over during her Wicca study, that first step was always the most difficult. But now that she'd begun, she was confident that she would succeed.

It was a little harder to maintain that feeling of confidence when she walked into Ms. Ableman's classroom the next period. Ever since the incident with Sherrie, Ms. Ableman had regarded Kate with a distinctly suspicious attitude. Where before she had always said hello to Kate, now she simply nodded when Kate entered the room. Kate took her seat and pretended to be looking through her text-book—anything to keep her gaze away from her teacher. She hated having people think badly of her, and she knew Ms. Ableman had most definitely put Kate into the troublemaker category. Kate wished there was some way she could make up for what she'd done—particularly where her grade was concerned.

The bell rang and Ms. Ableman shut the classroom door. She stood behind her desk, a stack of papers in her hand. Looking at them, Kate could tell they were the lab project reports that everyone had handed in the week before—everyone, that is, except for her and Sherrie. She glanced over at Sherrie and saw that she was completely focused on examining her cuticles. For the first time since their friendship ended, Kate felt like she and Sherrie were on the same wavelength.

"I've read all of your reports," Ms. Ableman said. "Some of them were very good."

There was a collective sigh from the students surrounding Kate. They all knew that their lab reports were a crucial part of their grades, and she knew that a lot of people had been afraid of failing. Now Kate saw relieved smiles on many faces.

"And many of them weren't good," Ms. Ableman continued.

A lot of the smiles faded, and Kate noticed an air of tension settling over the class again. She knew everyone was wondering who the unlucky ones were. *At least I don't have to wonder*, she thought, without any sense of relief.

"As you're all aware, the testing portion of your grade counts for one half, the other half being based on participation and lab assignments. A failing grade on this lab report means trouble for some of you." She looked pointedly at Kate when she said this, making Kate blush with shame.

"Because of this, I've decided that those of you who failed this assignment may do a makeup experiment."

Once again a sigh of relief rose up from the students. Some actually threw their hands in the air in thanks, while others closed their eyes in silent thank-yous. Kate wanted to join them, but she wasn't sure that she was included in the group who would be allowed to do a makeup project. After all, she'd gotten a failing grade not because she hadn't done the experiment properly, but because she'd turned the lab into a mud wrestling arena for her battle with Sherrie. Would Ms. Ableman relent and let her do another experiment?

"*All* of you who received failing grades may do another experiment," the teacher said, looking at Kate and then at Sherrie meaningfully. "However, there is one condition."

Whatever it is, it's fine with me, Kate thought as happiness flooded through her. Her day was getting better and better. First she'd discovered what was probably the clue to figuring out her challenge.

Now she was being given a chance to bring her grade in science back up. Clearly, things were going her way.

"You will be given a different experiment to perform," continued Ms. Ableman.

No biggie, Kate thought. She could handle another experiment. She could have handled the *first* one if Sherrie hadn't screwed it up.

"And you will work with the same partner you worked with last time," finished Ms. Ableman. She looked at Kate, and Kate was certain that she saw a smile of triumph on her teacher's face.

How could she? she thought. *How could she make me work with Sherrie again? Especially after what happened?* Surely the teacher had to be kidding. There was no way she could make Kate team up with Sherrie again. No way. She looked at Ms. Ableman in horror, but the teacher simply looked away.

"Those of you who wish to do the makeup project can see me after class," she said as she began handing back the papers. "If you don't wish to take it, that's your choice. You can accept your failing grade and hope that by some miracle you receive nothing but As on the remaining ones."

Kate glanced over at Sherrie just in time to see Sherrie turn away. *She was looking at me, too,* Kate thought. She knew that Sherrie had to be just as horrified at the prospect of teaming up again as Kate was. Maybe even more, since Kate had won their battle. What would happen if one of them

24

said no to the offer? Would Ms. Ableman assign the remaining girl a new partner, or would the whole deal be off? Kate was worried; it would be just like Sherrie to say she wouldn't do it, just to get even. But Sherrie couldn't afford to fail the class, either, not if she wanted to stay on the cheerleading squad. And being on the squad was the most important thing in Sherrie's life. *Except for making other people miserable*, thought Kate.

Class seemed to drag on and on. Finally it ended, and Kate hung back as other people left. She wasn't alone. At least a dozen people were milling around Ms. Ableman's desk, sheepish looks on their faces. Kate noticed, with a strange sense of relief, that Sherrie was among them, although she didn't make a move to come over and talk to Kate.

Kate let everyone else go ahead of her, until finally just she and Sherrie remained. The two of them stood as far away from each other as they could and waited for Ms. Ableman to say something.

The teacher looked from one to the other.

"I hope the two of you know how lucky you are," she said. "I wasn't going to let you do a makeup project. But I decided to give you a chance. *One* chance," she added, with emphasis. "If anything happens like what happened the last time, both of you fail. And not just this test, the whole class."

Kate felt a knot forming in her stomach. But all

she did was nod. Sherrie did the same.

"Okay," Ms. Ableman said, handing them each several sheets of paper stapled together. "Here's your new assignment. Note that it does *not* involve dirt. You have three weeks."

Kate looked at the handout. The experiment they'd been assigned seemed pretty easy. But there was still Sherrie to think about. Could Kate really work with her after what had happened? *You have to*, she told herself.

Kate nodded her thanks at Ms. Ableman and left the room. Sherrie followed her. Only when they were both in the hallway did they look at one another.

"I'm only doing this because I have to," Sherrie said coldly.

"No kidding," replied Kate. "Let's just do it and get it over with."

"Fine," Sherrie said.

"Fine," said Kate.

The two of them glared at each other and then turned and walked in opposite directions. They hadn't even made any plans for divvying up the work, but Kate didn't care. They could worry about it later. The important thing was that—awful as the prospect of having to talk to Sherrie again was— she'd been given a second chance.

By the time ninth period rolled around, she'd calmed down about the Sherrie thing. She would just have to grin and bear it. At least she had New

Orleans to look forward to. A week away from Beecher Falls was just what she needed. She would come back rested and ready to take on Sherrie and the experiment.

But first she needed to get started on her challenge. She headed for the library, where she went right for the folklore and fairy tale books. She didn't really know where to begin, so she decided to get one of everything. She grabbed a complete volume of the Brothers Grimm, something called *Hero Quests and Journeys*, a book on gods and goddesses from around the world, and individual collections of Norse, Greek, American Indian, and Russian folk tales. *This is a good start*, she thought, knowing that it was about as much as she could carry in her backpack.

She took the books to the circulation desk and checked them out. Then she sat at a table and began skimming through the various volumes, looking for clues. The stories were fascinating, and she found herself becoming involved in one about a boy who found a sailing ship that could fold up and fit in his pocket. Before she realized how much time had gone by, the bell rang and it was time to go home. Gathering up her books, she left the library and went to her locker for her coat.

Kate was looking forward to getting home. She had very little homework to do, and she was anxious to spend more time with the books she'd checked out. Even the idea of working with Sherrie on their makeup experiment didn't seem quite as terrible as it had earlier, and she was feeling good about her life.

When she reached her house she headed immediately for the kitchen. She could smell cookies baking, and the scent of vanilla and cinnamon drew her into the room, where she found her mother sliding cookies from a baking sheet to cooling trays with a spatula.

"Hey," Kate said, reaching for a cookie. "These smell great."

Her mother smiled tightly at her, causing Kate to pause.

"What?" she said. "Did something happen?"

Her mother turned and picked up something from the counter, which she held up. It was a white envelope. "This came today," she said.

Kate took the proffered envelope and looked at it. It was from her school. Immediately she knew what it was—her grades.

"I can explain," Kate said. "See . . ."

"I know what happened, Kate," Mrs. Morgan said. "I spoke to your teacher this afternoon. She explained everything. I convinced her to let you do a makeup project."

So that's why she gave in, Kate thought. The very idea that her mother had asked her teacher to give her another chance made her sick to her stomach. Especially since her mother hadn't known anything about the fight with Sherrie.

"I wanted to tell you," Kate said helplessly.

"But you didn't," said Mrs. Morgan.

Kate looked down at the floor. "I'm sorry," she said.

"I'm sure you are," her mother replied. "But that doesn't change the fact that you didn't tell us what was going on."

"Does Dad know?" asked Kate.

Her mother nodded, and the sick feeling in Kate's stomach doubled. She knew that her father would be even more upset than her mother was. *Why didn't I tell them?* she asked herself. It would have been difficult, but not as difficult as this was.

"Your father doesn't think you should go to New Orleans," said her mother.

Kate's head jerked up. "What?" she said, not believing what she was hearing.

"He thinks you should stay here and work on your makeup project," her mother continued.

"But I have three weeks to do that!" protested Kate. "We're only going to New Orleans for a week. I have to go! I've been looking forward to this."

Her mother leaned against the counter. "I know you have," she said. "I know you want to go with your friends. But I agree with your father on this one, Kate. I think you should stay here."

Kate's mouth hung open. She was speechless.

She couldn't even say anything in her defense. It was as if she were in the middle of a bad dream—the worst dream imaginable—and couldn't wake up. All she could do was stare at her mother, tears forming in her eyes. She wasn't going to New Orleans.

CHAPTER 3

"What do you mean you're not going?" Cooper stared at Kate in disbelief.

"I'm not going," repeated Kate. "My parents said no."

"You've got to be kidding," said Annie. "Please tell us you're kidding."

Kate groaned. "Would I kid about something like this?" she asked. "They said no way."

She leaned against the wall by Cooper's locker, where they had all met up on Thursday morning. All the way to school she'd been trying to figure out how to break the bad news. Finally she'd just blurted it out. Now that she'd done it, she felt like crying. It was like telling her friends made it official or something, and she had to accept the fact that while they were living it up in New Orleans, she was going to be in snowy, cold Beecher Falls doing a makeup experiment with the one person on Earth she would rather die than have to work with.

Cooper and Annie weren't saying anything,

which made it worse. Kate had been hoping they would make her feel better somehow. But there really wasn't anything they could say that would help. It was her own fault that she wasn't going to be getting on a plane with them on Friday afternoon, her fault and nobody else's.

Cooper shook her head. "This really bites," she said. She looked at Kate. "It *really* bites."

"You don't have to tell me," Kate responded. "I'm the one who's getting bitten, remember? I just wish that letter had waited a few more days."

"I know this probably won't help," Annie said, "but maybe there's a reason you need to be here. I mean, maybe this happened for a reason."

"Yeah," Kate said. "It happened because I had to go and get all WWF on Sherrie."

"That's not what I mean," Annie said. "I mean maybe this is part of your challenge."

Kate and Cooper looked at her with doubtful expressions.

"What?" Annie said. "It could be. Look at all the other stuff that's happened to us that looked bad when it happened but turned out to be something good."

"Sherrie could *never* be something good," commented Kate, and Cooper nodded in agreement.

"I'm with Kate on that one," said Cooper. "This just blows, plain and simple."

The first bell rang. "Well, we'll have to talk about it later," Annie said as they prepared to go to class. "And don't forget—tonight is Sasha's birthday dinner."

They split up and went to their respective classes, Kate to English, Annie to Spanish, and Cooper to math. Cooper walked into Mr. Niemark's room and took her seat. Just as Kate had done the day before, Cooper spent more time scribbling in her notebook than she did listening to Mr. Niemark's lecture. But in Cooper's case, she was busily writing lyrics, not making lists. She and Jane—who together made up the band the Bitter Pills—were working on a bunch of new material. Ever since Jane had come out as a lesbian, she'd been in this phenomenal creative period, churning out song after song. Cooper, who couldn't help but feel a little competitive, was having a hard time keeping up. *Maybe I should become a lesbian, too*, she thought, laughing to herself.

As she wrote, she thought about Kate. It really was too bad that Kate wasn't going to be coming to New Orleans with her and Annie. Cooper had really been looking forward to spending some time with her friends away from home. The two other times they'd gone away together—once camping in the woods at Midsummer and then on a retreat at Yule—they'd wound up in some strange adventures. It would be nice just to have a regular vacation.

Besides, Annie was primarily going to New Orleans to see her sister. They would probably want to spend some time together by themselves.

That left Cooper all by herself. With Kate along, she would have had someone to explore the city with. Now she was going to be on her own. Normally that would be fine with her, but she'd gotten so used to thinking that she would be doing things with other people that now she felt a little bit lost imagining doing them on her own.

Then there was her challenge. She had managed to put that out of her mind. Now it was back, and she realized that one of the reasons she'd been looking forward to being in New Orleans with her friends was because she was worried about her challenge. She hadn't let on to anyone that she was concerned about it, but the truth was that she was more than a little apprehensive about getting started on it.

She looked down at her notebook and realized that she'd stopped writing lyrics and instead was writing her challenge over and over. "Face the thing you fear the most," was written repeatedly over five lines of the page. She was in the middle of writing it again, with "Face the thing" being the last words she'd written. Now she lifted her pen from the page and just stared at the words. "Face the thing you fear the most." When she'd seen those words on her slip of paper on Tuesday night, she'd felt lucky. Facing a fear seemed very concrete, something she could visualize and push her way through. She had always been pretty good at facing things she was afraid of, and she'd felt confident that this time would be no different.

But the more she thought about it, the harder she realized her challenge was. First of all, she had to figure out what it was she was most afraid of. Her initial thought had been sharks. Silly as it seemed, she was terrified of sharks. Ever since she'd seen *Jaws* on TV when she was six, she'd been afraid of the big fish, not really because of their killing power but because she hated the idea that there were things swimming around under the water that she couldn't see. Little fish and things like turtles and lobsters and other sea creatures didn't bother her at all. But the idea that something as big as a shark could be swimming around underneath her, ready to pop its ugly head up at any moment, freaked her out. She rarely ventured into the ocean ever since, and then for very short periods of time.

She doubted, though, that her challenge had anything to do with great whites or makos. Magic was usually more subtle than that. And that's what bothered her. Only once had she really been afraid of her involvement in Wicca—during the ritual they'd attended for the Summer Solstice. That was when she'd been essentially kidnapped and terrorized by a group of kids claiming to be faeries. They'd led Cooper on a strange chase through the woods, a chase where she'd been forced to play the part of the hunted animal. It had unnerved her, coming that close to such wild, untamed magic, and she'd temporarily left the group because she hadn't been able to handle her emotions about what had happened to her.

She'd come back to Wicca eventually, but the memories of that night still lingered in her mind. She feared that perhaps her challenge had something to do with that night in the woods and what happened afterward. But hadn't she already faced that fear? Wasn't it behind her? She'd certainly believed that it was. But she couldn't imagine what else she might still be afraid of. Except the sharks. They were still around.

She sighed. Sometimes magic was really frustrating. It didn't always behave by the rules, at least not by any rules she could figure out. Of course, that's also what she loved about it. She herself didn't always play by the rules. In fact, she almost never played by the rules. That had been her attraction to witchcraft in the first place. Having studied magic for almost a year now—and having experienced its often-fickle nature—she understood a little better why sometimes the people in her life found her difficult to understand. She just wished she understood her challenge a little bit better. She was willing to face her fear, at least she thought she was. But first she had to figure out what it was.

She had no way of knowing that Kate, sitting only a few desks away from where Cooper now sat, had made a list of potentially unanswerable questions. Now it was Cooper's turn to make a list.

Below the lines covered with "Face the thing you fear the most," she hastily scrawled:

Things I'm Afraid Of
  1. Sharks
  2. Mom or Dad dying
  3. Losing T.J.

That was all she could come up with. The second two items were things she hadn't really thought about before, but now they came to her easily. Still, she didn't think they really counted. Magic could be tough sometimes, but she knew she would never be asked to confront those things as part of a test. *But Annie had to,* she told herself, thinking about how the deaths of Annie's parents had played a huge part in her understanding of magic and her growth in Wicca. That was different, though. Mr. and Mrs. Crandall had died long before Annie had become interested in witchcraft. Magic had had nothing to do with it.

No, she was certain that neither her parents nor her relationship with T.J. was in jeopardy. *That leaves sharks,* she thought. *Maybe I'm going to fall off a boat and be surrounded by sharks. Then I'll have to use magic to make their teeth fall out.* She laughed at the absurdity of the idea. It sounded like something out of Harry Potter. Then again, sometimes she wished magic was as easy as it was in those books. While she would never admit it, and in fact would probably deny it if asked, she loved reading Harry Potter. The way magic was portrayed in the stories was how she'd always thought of magic when she was little. Now she knew better, but still it was fun to read about a world where people could make things happen just by waving a wand.

The bell rang. Cooper closed her notebook. There was time to think about her challenge later. First she had to get through the rest of the day. And then there was Sasha's party that night. As she left to go to her next class, she tried to think of something they could do to cheer up Kate. They couldn't make up for the disappointment of her not being able to go to New Orleans, but maybe they could help ease the blow a little.

That night, a little before seven o'clock, Cooper arrived at Annie's house. She was carrying two wrapped gifts. When she went inside, she found Annie in the kitchen, putting the finishing touches on a chocolate cake.

"Is Kate here yet?" Cooper asked, looking around.

Annie shook her head. "No," she said. "You're the first one."

"Good," said Cooper. She set the two presents on the table. "I brought her a present." She held up one of the boxes. It was quite large, and when she shook it, it rattled.

"What is it?" Annie asked.

Cooper gave her a mysterious look. "You'll have to wait to find out," she said. "It's a care package. Stuff for Kate to remember us with while we're gone."

"Don't you think she'd rather forget us?" asked Annie.

"I'm just trying to cheer her up," said Cooper.

"I know," Annie said. "I'm sure she'll love it— whatever it is."

"You seem a little tense," remarked Cooper, sticking her finger in the frosting Annie was using and tasting it.

"I guess I'm just a little nervous," Annie admitted. "I'm going to meet my sister tomorrow. It feels weird."

"It will be *fun*," Cooper said.

"I know," Annie said. "But what if she doesn't like me? What if I don't like her?"

Annie should have gotten my challenge, thought Cooper as she listened to her friend talk. It occurred to her that Annie really was facing one of her worst fears in meeting her sister. If things didn't go well, it wasn't like she could just forget about Juliet. She would always know she was out there, and that they were related. Thinking about that made Cooper's worries about her own challenge seem unimportant. But what *was* Annie's challenge? she wondered. Since she hadn't chosen the one about facing her fears, Cooper couldn't imagine what she *had* chosen. Was it something even more difficult? She was dying to ask Annie, but she knew it was against the rules.

Besides, before they could talk anymore about it, the front door opened and Kate arrived with Sasha. They had decided to limit the get-together to the four of them because Annie and Cooper—and formerly Kate—had to leave the next day for New Orleans. Technically, it wasn't even really Sasha's birthday; that was on the fourth. But since her friends were going to be away, they'd decided to celebrate early.

"Hey, birthday girl," said Cooper, giving Sasha a big hug.

"Sorry I'm a little late," said Sasha. "Mallory called, and I wanted to find out what was going on."

"How is she?" asked Annie. Mallory, like Sasha, had been a runaway. She'd come to Beecher Falls the month before, running from an old boyfriend who wanted to harm her. The guy had shown up and beaten Mallory, and the girls had helped her out. They'd been able to reunite her with her brother, Derek, and now Mallory was living with him and his wife in Maine.

"She's doing really well," said Sasha happily. "She's about to go back to school, which will be a big deal for her. She's missed a lot, but she says she's determined to graduate. I'm really proud of her."

"Now if we could just keep that creep Ray in jail, we'd be all set," remarked Cooper angrily, referring to the old boyfriend who had attacked Mallory and then tried to attack them when they'd stopped him.

"Oh, that's the best part," Sasha said. "The police called Mallory a few days ago. Because of what she told them, they've managed to connect Ray to a whole bunch of crimes, including a murder in L.A. With any luck, he'll never get out."

Cooper gave Sasha a celebratory high five. "Way to go," she said. "So, how does it feel to be turning sixteen?"

Sasha was the last of their group of friends to turn the magic number. Kate's had been the most recent birthday, back in January. Annie and Cooper had turned sixteen the previous year. In fact, Cooper was looking ahead to turning seventeen at the end of April.

"Finally I'm catching up," Sasha said. "Now I don't feel like the baby anymore. I mean, I know I still am, but at least it doesn't feel that way. What's this?" she added, picking up one of the boxes Cooper had set on the table.

"Not yet," Cooper said, taking it away from her. "Cake and festivities first. And Kate, this box is for you."

"Me?" Kate said. "What did I do?"

"It's just for being you," Cooper said, pushing

the box toward her friend. "Go on. Open it."

"Hey," Sasha said. "It's *my* birthday party. How come she gets to open a present?"

"Because I said so," Cooper replied. "Kate is before cake; you're after cake."

Kate pulled the paper from the box and lifted the lid. She reached in and pulled out another, smaller box. It too was wrapped, and it was numbered 4. She looked at it, puzzled, then reached in and pulled out another box. This one was marked with a number 1.

"There are seven of them," said Cooper. "One for every day Annie and I are gone. You can only open one at a time."

Kate picked up package number 1 and felt it. "Is it a book?" she asked curiously.

"Put it back!" Cooper ordered her. "You are *not* to open that until Saturday."

"But that isn't fair!" wailed Kate. "First I don't get to go with you, and now you won't let me open the presents. You are so mean."

"Hey, I got you presents, didn't I?" Cooper told her, grinning.

Kate smiled. Then she hugged her friend. "Thanks," she said. "I can't say it's better than going to New Orleans, but it makes it easier having to stay here alone. I can't wait to see what these things are. You promise they aren't just empty boxes, right?"

"Who's to say?" Cooper replied cryptically.

"And by the way, you won't be here all by your-self," Sasha said to Kate. "I'll be here. Now you'll get to be around for my real birthday. Let them have New Orleans," she said, putting her arm around Kate and facing Cooper and Annie. "*We* are going to have big birthday fun."

"Right," Kate said in agreement, although she sounded a little unsure.

"Speaking of big birthday fun, let's get going on this cake," said Annie. She had lit the sixteen candles on the cake, and now she set the whole thing in front of Sasha. "Put your lips together and blow," she ordered. "And don't forget to make a wish."

Sasha leaned forward and puffed heavily. The candles flickered and then went out, thin streams of smoke drifting toward the ceiling. "That's one wish granted," she said, pumping her fist. "Want to know what it was?"

"You're not supposed to tell," Annie chided her as she cut the cake.

"It's my birthday," replied Sasha. "I'll tell if I want to. I wished you all would pass your challenges with flying colors."

Annie, Cooper, and Kate looked at one another, each wondering what the other two thought of Sasha's wish.

"Using your wish for us," Cooper said. "How very unselfish."

"That's just the kind of girl I am," Sasha said,

taking the plate Annie handed her and digging into the piece of cake. "Besides, I'll get another wish on my actual birthday. *That* one is going to be all about me. And Josh Hartnett," she added, licking frosting from her lips. "Now where are those presents?"

CHAPTER 4

Annie looked over at Cooper. She was asleep. Her headphones were on and her mouth was open as she dozed. Annie wished she could sleep, too, but she'd never been able to nap on airplanes. Besides, she was too excited. In just a short time she was going to meet her big sister for the first time. She checked her watch for what seemed like the thousandth time since they'd taken off five hours before. They would be landing within the hour, and the closer the time came the more nervous Annie got.

Then she looked at the empty seat between herself and Cooper. Kate should have been occupying it. Instead, she was back in Beecher Falls. Annie was sad that her friend couldn't be with them. But she was trying not to let that get in the way of how happy she was to be meeting Juliet. She thought about the gifts Aunt Sarah and Meg had helped her put together—the photo album of pictures of their parents, the video they'd had made of some home movies Peter Crandall had taken, and the painting that Chloe Crandall had done. That last item was packed carefully and was sitting at the front of the plane. Annie had convinced them not to make her check it, and one of the flight attendants had put it in a safe place. Annie had selected the painting from among those her aunt had stored. It was a picture of a black dog sitting in a garden. The dog was surrounded by purple irises, and Annie loved the contrasting colors. She didn't know why, but she thought Juliet might like it as well.

She turned back to the window, looking out at the black sky. Even though they'd left school halfway through the day to take an early flight, it was still evening because of the time difference. Outside the plane stars twinkled brightly in the darkness, and the red lights on the plane's wings blinked steadily. Annie looked down, wondering if she could see any lights from below, but nothing was visible through the thick clouds.

She leaned back and closed her eyes, trying to at least relax a little. She didn't want to be too exhausted on her first night in New Orleans. But she was simply too worked up to rest. Besides, there was something weighing on her mind. That was her challenge. While her approaching meeting with Juliet had occupied most of her waking thoughts, the challenge was lurking in the background. She knew she was going to have to deal with it sooner rather than later.

What troubled her was that she thought maybe

she'd chosen the wrong one. The slip she'd taken from the Challenge Box told her "Give away your most precious possession." Seeing the instruction, Annie had at first thought it was a straightforward challenge. She simply had to give away something she owned. But as she'd thought more about it, the more confused she'd become. She didn't really have anything that was worth a lot of money, except perhaps for her computer. And technically that belonged to Aunt Sarah, who had paid for it. Annie herself owned almost nothing of monetary value.

Then she'd thought that maybe the thing she had to give away was something with personal value. She had a lot of that kind of thing, including the paintings her mother had done, the photographs of her family that helped her remember them, and the various magical gifts Kate and Cooper had given her. Perhaps, she thought, her challenge was to give one of those things away.

But that wasn't much of a challenge. As much as she cherished those things, she would be able to give them away without too much trouble if she really had to. They were, after all, just *things*. And anyway, she didn't think that Sophia and the others who had written the challenges would expect her to give away something like a photo of her parents to prove that she was ready to become a witch. That was more like something someone would be asked to do to join a stupid gang, or a sorority or something where they wanted to embarrass you. Wicca didn't require

47

people to do meaningless things like that. Annie just couldn't make sense of her challenge.

At least it didn't make sense for *her*. But maybe it made sense for someone else in the class. After all, each person's challenge was supposed to be uniquely theirs. What was it Sophia had said? They didn't choose the challenges so much as the challenges chose them. Was it possible that Annie had somehow taken a slip meant for someone else? Would the words mean something important to another person in the class? But wouldn't Sophia or Archer have noticed something when they saw what she'd selected? She'd been tempted to go back later and ask them if she could choose again, but that had seemed like breaking the rules.

Annie sighed. *Maybe you need to break the rules more often*, she told herself glumly. She wanted to be excited about her challenge. Instead, she just felt confused. If it *did* belong to someone else, she would just be wasting her time trying to complete it. And what if someone else had *her* challenge? Then two people would be doing the wrong thing.

Well, she couldn't really worry about it now. She was thousands of miles from home and from the store. She would have to deal with it when she got back. She would just go to Sophia and tell her that the challenge wasn't right for her. Surely, Sophia would understand that. It would all work out fine in the end, Annie told herself.

"Ladies and gentlemen, we will be landing in New

Orleans in approximately twenty-five minutes. Please fasten your seat belts in preparation for arrival." The announcement came over the plane's speakers. Annie leaned over and patted Cooper's arm. Her friend opened her eyes and looked around sleepily.

"What?" Cooper said, sounding confused. "Is it time for school? Just fifteen more minutes." She started to close her eyes again. Then she saw Annie watching her and she sat up. "Are we there?"

"Almost," Annie said.

Cooper stretched and yawned while Annie busied herself collecting everything she'd spread out on the seat beside her and returned it to her backpack. Within minutes she was all ready to disembark. Cooper, meanwhile, was still searching for the shoes she'd removed before falling asleep. But after a few minutes of rooting around under her seat she, too, had gathered her things and was waiting expectantly to land.

As the plane descended, Annie kept stealing glances out the window, as if perhaps if she looked hard enough she could somehow see Juliet below them. She wondered if Juliet was looking up at some blinking red lights in the sky and hoping they belonged to Annie's plane.

Soon she could see the lights of the city beneath them, and then the runway lights as the plane approached the airport. When she felt the wheels touch down, she thought she might not be able to sit still another minute longer. Juliet was right inside the terminal, waiting for her.

It seemed to take forever for the plane to taxi down the runway and pull up to the gate. Annie kept watching the seat belt sign, and as soon as it went off she unbuckled herself and stood up. Cooper stepped into the aisle and opened the overhead luggage compartment, removing their bags. Annie took hers and immediately headed for the front of the plane. When she had to stop because there were people ahead of her, she tapped her fingers on the back of a seat impatiently.

"Relax," Cooper said. "We'll be there in a minute."

Annie tried to follow her friend's advice, but she just couldn't. Every second seemed like an eternity, and she kept craning her neck around the other passengers to see what was taking so long. Finally the line began to move, and a minute later they were at the front of the plane. A flight attendant handed Annie the painting that had been stored there.

"Thanks," Annie said as she stepped into the gangway. Immediately she was hit with a blast of hot, moist air.

"Whew," said Cooper, coming out behind her. "That must be the swamp. Goddess, it's hot."

"Come on," Annie said, storming ahead in her rush to get inside. Cooper followed along behind, saying "Excuse us" as Annie moved by the slower passengers.

As soon as they stepped into the terminal, Annie scanned the area for Juliet. She found her almost immediately. She was standing near the gate, holding a big hand-lettered sign that said CRANDALL FAMILY REUNION. When she saw Annie and Cooper, she waved.

Now that she was actually face-to-face with her sister, Annie didn't know what to do. For a moment she just stood there, staring at Juliet and praying she wouldn't wake up and find out it was a dream.

"Go on," said Cooper gently. "Say hello to your big sis."

Annie ran to Juliet, who dropped the sign she was holding and held out her arms. Annie ran into them, and as soon as they closed around her she began to cry tears of happiness.

"You look just like your picture," she said, her voice shaking. She kept running her hands over Juliet's back, making sure she was real.

"So do you," said Juliet, stroking Annie's hair.

They stayed that way for a long time, neither saying anything. Annie tried to take in everything so that she could remember it—the way Juliet's hair felt, the citrusy scent of her perfume, the feel of her body. Then, too soon, they pulled apart and stood looking at one another.

"I'm sorry I'm staring," Juliet said after a minute of standing there looking at Annie in silence. "It's just that I've never seen anyone who looks like me. My brothers and sisters don't look anything like me."

"We look like Dad," Annie told her. "Meg looks more like Mom. But you and I have Dad's nose."

Juliet hugged her again. "I just can't believe you're really here," she said. "I can't wait to show you New Orleans."

"And we can't wait to see it," remarked Cooper, who had been standing a little way off and giving the sisters some time to greet each other.

"I'm Cooper," she said now, shaking Juliet's hand.

"Annie's told me so much about you," replied Juliet. Then she turned to Annie. "I don't think she looks like trouble at all."

"Hey!" Cooper exclaimed. "Just what did you tell her?" she demanded of Annie.

"Just the truth," answered Annie, winking.

Juliet took one of the bags from Cooper and the three of them walked away from the gate. Annie kept stealing glances at her sister, trying to memorize everything about her. It was amazing to her how similar the two of them were, and it felt really strange to be walking through the airport with someone she hadn't even known about a few months before but who was now family to her. She was surprised to discover that she didn't even feel nervous now that she was actually with Juliet. It felt like she was reuniting with her after a trip away or something. She wondered if Juliet felt the same way.

As they exited the doors of the airport they were once again hit with the hot, steamy air. Annie breathed it in deeply, soaking in the earthy, wet scent that was so different from the crisp, dry air of Beecher Falls, which normally smelled like ocean and pine trees. There was something mysterious about the smell of New Orleans, something that felt old, sleepy, and filled with possibilities waiting to be discovered.

"Is it always like this?" asked Cooper as they walked to Juliet's car.

Juliet laughed. "Sometimes it's hotter," she said. "And wetter. Don't forget, we're basically in a swamp. New Orleans is actually *below* sea level, so it's very humid. But you get used to it. Besides, there's something mysterious about it, don't you think? I fell in love with the place the very first time I came."

Annie smiled to herself when she heard Juliet's words. It made her feel good to know that she and her sister thought the same way about things, even if it was something as small as what the air smelled like.

Reaching Juliet's car, they put the bags in the trunk, slid the painting into the back along with Cooper, and then Annie got in front with Juliet. As they drove out of the airport, Annie remarked on the large number of people pouring out of the terminals.

"That's Mardi Gras," Juliet said. "This town goes insane this time of year. In fact, a lot of residents actually go on vacation for a few weeks until it's over. If you think the airport is bad, wait until we get into the actual city."

As they drove along the highway into town, Juliet told them a little bit about herself and how she'd ended up in New Orleans.

"I came here with some friends on a trip," she said. "And like I said before, I fell in love with the place. It's like nowhere else in the world. The people, the music, the food—it's all incredible. I went back and told my parents that I wanted to go to school here. They were *not* thrilled. My father wanted me to go to business school. My mother didn't care what I did, but she didn't want me too far away. But I badgered them endlessly until they agreed to let me come here. I've been here ever since."

"Annie said you work as a costume designer," said Cooper.

"That's right," Juliet replied. "I work for the Night Vision Theater. They do all kinds of things, from Shakespeare to experimental stuff. They're really popular here, and they're particularly known for their elaborate stage sets and their costumes. Everything they do is a spectacle."

"I'd love to see some of your costumes," said Annie.

"You'll get your chance," Juliet told her. "We're putting on a production for Mardi Gras. Plus, I've been designing the costumes for one of the krewes."

"One of the what?" asked Cooper.

"Krewes," Juliet repeated. "That's what they call the individual groups who build floats for the Mardi Gras parade. Some of the krewes have been in existence for years and years. I'm designing the costumes for one of them."

"What's the theme of the float?" Annie inquired.

"That's the cool part," Juliet told her. "It's all about voodoo."

"Voodoo?" Annie said, intrigued.

"I'm sure you know voodoo is one of New Orleans's most famous products," Juliet said, laughing. "Thanks to Marie Laveau."

"Who?" Cooper asked.

"Marie Laveau," Juliet repeated. "The voodoo queen of New Orleans. She's famous."

"More famous than Anne Rice?" Cooper said.

"Please," Juliet answered. "Anne Rice only *wishes* she was as famous as Marie Laveau. Anne may own half of the city now, but Marie *ruled* it when she was alive. People were either terrified of her or in love with her. They say she had incredible powers and could do all kinds of magic."

"She sounds like our kind of girl, huh, Annie?" Cooper said.

Annie nodded but didn't say anything. She had never discussed her involvement in Wicca with Juliet, and she didn't want to spoil what was so far a great first meeting by bringing up something that was potentially dangerous. Juliet was talking about voodoo and magic as if they were perfectly ordinary, so maybe she would be okay with it, but Annie wasn't quite ready to risk it.

"We can take the voodoo tour while you're here," said Juliet. "It's a lot of fun. I mean, I'm sure most of it is total legend, but it's fun anyway."

They had reached the city, and now Juliet was navigating the car through some narrow streets. Annie looked around them as they drove, taking it all in. The buildings were old. Almost all of them were made of brick or stucco, and they all looked like something out of a movie. The streetlights were the old-fashioned kind, and they added to the feeling that they had somehow stepped back in time. Annie half expected to see horse-drawn carriages come around the corners, or people in top hats and hoop skirts walking on the sidewalks.

There *were* people. Lots of people. They walked right in the streets. They sat on balconies. They leaned in doorways. Annie had never seen so many people just hanging out. It was as if there was a gigantic party going on and the whole city had been invited.

"It's insane even trying to drive during Mardi Gras," said Juliet. "Once we park this thing I'm not taking it out again until this is all over."

She turned down another street and stopped at a wrought-iron gate. She gave a honk and a moment later a girl appeared. She looked at the car, waved, and then opened the gate to let Juliet drive in. Juliet crossed a cobblestone courtyard and drove the car into what looked like a small barn.

"This used to be the stable for the horses," she said as she parked. "Now it's our garage."

They got out of the car. The girl who had opened the gate came up to them. "Hi," she said. "I'm Darcy."

"Darcy is one of my roommates," Juliet said. "This is Cooper," she told Darcy. Then she put her arm around Annie. "And this is my little sister."

"Welcome to New Orleans," said Darcy. She was tall and slender, with short red hair and pale skin. She was dressed in a black velvet dress that looked like something out of a Gothic romance novel.

"Cool dress," Cooper said, noting it.

"This is one of the costumes for the show," Darcy explained. "I'm not usually this dramatic. We were just hemming it."

"Are you a costume designer, too?" Annie asked.

"Costume designer, actor, writer—you name it," Darcy replied. "We tend to do it all around here, otherwise nothing gets done."

"Speaking of getting done," Juliet said. "Let's get you guys settled. Then we're going out to dinner to celebrate your arrival."

"Isn't it a little late?" asked Annie, looking at her watch and seeing that it was almost eleven already.

Darcy and Juliet laughed. "New Orleans never

closes," Juliet said as she picked up a bag and led the girls toward the house. "Especially not during Mardi Gras."

Cooper and Annie followed the other girls. As they crossed the courtyard Annie heard the sound of a brass band playing somewhere beyond the gate. It was almost as if they were playing a welcome song for Annie and Cooper.

"I think we are going to have a *great* time here," she said to Cooper.

CHAPTER 5

Kate woke up on Saturday morning wishing she were dead. It was the first day of break, but it felt like anything but. Not only was she not in New Orleans with her friends, but she had to spend the week working on her science project with Sherrie. What could be worse than that?

She looked out the window of her bedroom and saw the answer to that question. It was raining. Snow she could handle. Snow was pretty, and it was kind of fun to walk around in. Rain was a different story. Rain was wet and cold and miserable, particularly in winter. Now it was raining steadily. Everything outside looked gray and depressing, which made Kate feel even worse than she already did.

She pulled the covers over her head and closed her eyes. *Maybe I can just stay here all day,* she thought. That wasn't such a bad thing. It was warm under the covers, and she felt safe there. There was no Sherrie, no science experiment, no problems. It was like she had shut the whole world out and was all alone. The only problem was, she couldn't breathe.

She threw back the covers and sighed. Staying in bed wasn't the answer. She had to get up and face her day. Reluctantly, she put one foot over the side of the bed and forced herself to sit up. It was a monumental effort to keep her eyes open, let alone approach the idea of standing up and going to take a shower with anything even remotely resembling enthusiasm or motivation. *Maybe I can get away without showering*, she thought darkly, unwilling to give in to the demands of her usual morning ritual.

Then she caught sight of herself in the mirror over her dresser. Her hair was a mess. *The shower is definitely* not *out*, she conceded. Then she spied the box Cooper had given her at Sasha's birthday party. True to her promise, Kate hadn't opened it again since bringing it home. It sat on her desk, waiting for her. She stood up, shuffled wearily over to it, and carried it back to her bed. Sitting cross-legged beside the box, she lifted up the top and looked inside. There were the seven gifts, each one numbered.

Kate picked up box number 1. It was small, and when she shook it it rattled very slightly. Wondering what it might be, she ripped the paper off and looked. It was a cassette tape. She looked at the label, which read "Cooper's Surprise Mix Tape," and smiled. *Leave it to Cooper*, she thought. Wondering what exactly her friend had put on the tape, Kate got her tape player from her desk drawer and slipped the tape into it. She put the headphones on, hit play, and listened.

"Hey there," said Cooper's voice. "If you're listening to this when you're supposed to, it's Saturday morning. Assuming our plane didn't crash, Annie and I are in New Orleans. We wish you were here. But you're not, so here's some cool music to help you get through your first day without us. Enjoy."

Cooper's voice faded out and a song began. It was the Ramones singing "I Wanna Be Sedated." Kate laughed. Cooper was always playing old Ramones tapes in the car. Not only did the song remind Kate of good times with her friends, but it totally captured how she felt right at that moment. "Twenty-twenty-twenty-four hours to go-o-o," Joey Ramone sang. "I wanna be sedated." With its punk rock sound and humorous lyrics, the song was exactly what Kate needed to jump-start her day. She stood up and began dancing around the room as she gathered up the clothes she wanted to wear and prepared for her shower.

Twenty minutes later she was in the kitchen, getting herself some breakfast. She was still listening to Cooper's tape. The Ramones had been followed by Blink 182 and then Eve 6. Kate was having a good time listening to the songs Cooper had put together for her. It didn't make up for not being with her friends in New Orleans, but at least listening to the tape put her in a better mood.

Her father had already left for the sporting goods store he owned, but Mrs. Morgan was still home. Coming into the kitchen and seeing Kate dancing around, she looked at her daughter with a bemused expression. At first Kate didn't see her, and continued to shake her head and wave her spoon in the air as she ate her cereal. Then she caught sight of her mother standing in the doorway and she stopped, turning red. She switched off the tape and removed the headphones.

"Hey," she said. "I was just—"

"No, let me guess," her mother said. "You've taken up aerobics? Oh, no, you're taking interpretive dance at school?"

"Ha ha," said Kate. "No, it's just a tape that Cooper made me because I couldn't go with them."

Her mother smiled softly. "Kate, I know it doesn't seem fair that we told you that you couldn't go," said Mrs. Morgan.

"It's okay," Kate told her. "Really. I mean, I'm upset that I'm not with Cooper and Annie, but I'm upset at me, not at you and Dad. I should have told you about the science class thing."

"You *are* doing your makeup project this week, right?" Mrs. Morgan asked.

Kate nodded. "I'm meeting Sherrie at the library at ten," she said. "Our new project is about rocks."

"Rocks?" her mother repeated. "What about them?"

"We're supposed to write a report about how you can get information about a place by studying the different sedimentary layers in rocks from the area. Ms. Ableman gave us some rock samples from the area around Beecher Falls. We're supposed to do some research on how this area has changed geographically."

"That actually sounds sort of interesting," remarked Mrs. Morgan.

"Sort of," admitted Kate. "But not when you have to do it with Sherrie." Kate had—reluctantly—told her mother the whole story about getting into a wrestling match with Sherrie over their previous science project. Now Mrs. Morgan tried not to laugh as she said, "Well, just don't go hitting her with any of those rock samples. You could do *serious* damage."

Kate rolled her eyes. "Thanks for the vote of confidence," she said as she left the kitchen to finish getting ready.

An hour later she walked into the library of Jasper College. She was glad she didn't live too far from the school, as the walk through the rain had been less than inspiring. Despite the umbrella she'd carried, the rain had managed to get her pretty damp, and she was all too happy to shed her coat as soon as she could. She went upstairs to the science reference section of the library and looked for Sherrie. Not finding her, Kate selected a table near the windows and put her stuff down. The view outside was, like the walk, not exactly cheerful, but at least they wouldn't feel trapped inside, the way they would at a table without a view. Besides, now that she was inside again, Kate sort of liked the way the rain pattered against the glass.

Sitting down, Kate took out the materials Ms. Ableman had given them. Mostly the handouts consisted of diagrams of rock layers taken from samples found around Beecher Falls. The rocks themselves were actually nothing more than small samples so that the girls could get an idea of what the various layers looked like. They were supposed to research the different time periods represented by the rock samples and write a report about how they thought the geography of the land had changed over the years and why.

Kate looked at the first of the handouts. It was a cross section of rock from approximately ten thousand years before. The different layers of sediment were labeled, and there were photographs of several different plants whose outlines had been preserved when the leaves were pressed between the various layers. Kate found the pictures fascinating. In some ways it was like looking at a scrapbook someone had kept with mementos and memories. Only these memories were made of dirt and minerals.

Someone dropped a backpack on the table, making Kate jump. She looked up and saw Sherrie taking off her coat and putting it over the back of a chair across from Kate.

"Sorry I'm late," Sherrie said coolly. "I had to wait for my father to drive me. I wasn't about to walk in that rain." She ruffled her hair as if highlighting the unspoken meaning of her statement—she was far too special to risk getting wet. Kate saw Sherrie glance at her own rain-soaked jacket and give a self-satisfied smirk, as if Kate were somehow beneath her because she had walked to the library.

Kate merely nodded in response. She wasn't about to get into anything with Sherrie. This time the project was all about grades. Even if she had to do all of the work herself, Kate was determined to get an A. She wanted to show Ms. Ableman that she wasn't a total screwup. More than that, she wanted to prove it to her parents and herself. As far as she was concerned, Sherrie was simply an inconvenience.

"So, what is it we're doing?" Sherrie asked. "Rocks?" She snorted. "And I thought plants were boring."

"At least with nothing to grow, there's nothing to kill," Kate remarked, alluding to the fact that their last experiment had failed, at least in part, due to the fact that Sherrie had forgotten to water properly the seedlings they were supposed to be growing.

Sherrie gave her a disgusted look. "I'm not the one who threw a giant tantrum over a little mistake," she said.

"A little mistake!" exclaimed Kate. She prepared herself for giving Sherrie a piece of her mind. Then she stopped, took a breath, and said, "I think this will work best if we each take a different part of the project. What if I work on the oldest rocks and you can work on the more recent ones?"

"Whatever," Sherrie replied, reaching into her backpack and pulling out some eyeliner and a compact. She opened the compact and began to apply the makeup to her eyes.

"Mostly this is going to be a lot of research and putting clues together," Kate said. "We basically have to create a profile of Beecher Falls's history using rocks—or the area that became Beecher Falls, anyway."

Sherrie snorted. "First it was dirt, then there was a lot of ice, then there was more dirt," she said. "What's so hard about that?"

Kate put the handout down. "Look," she said. "I don't really care whether you help with this or not. If you want, I'll write the whole thing and we can just put both our names on it."

Sherrie snapped the top on her eyeliner and popped it back into her bag. "Right," she said. "So you can tell Ableman I didn't do anything? I don't think so."

"I won't tell her anything," said Kate. "I just need a good grade on this, and the easier it is to do, the better. So why don't you just go home and I'll take care of it?"

Sherrie regarded her for a minute before speaking. "I'll stay," she said. "I need a good grade, too, and I don't trust you. For all I know, you'll deliberately write something that's totally wrong."

Kate threw her hands in the air. "Fine," she said. "In that case, let's just get to work. We need to find some books about the geography of the Pacific Northwest. Can you do that?"

"Books," Sherrie said. "How hard can that be?" She got up and walked away. A minute later she came back. "And just where would these books *be*?" she asked, as if Kate had hidden them from her.

"Over there," Kate answered, pointing her in the right direction.

Sherrie went off to find some reference books while Kate continued to look at the handouts. She was becoming more and more interested in the photos of the various items that had been trapped between the layers of rock. In addition to the leaves, there were insects and small animals. There was even the impression of a bird skeleton. Kate stared at the photos. What would the area around Beecher Falls have been like all those thousands of years ago? What would it have been like to walk around the forests then?

She looked out the window. The rain was coming down even harder now. Beyond the buildings of Jasper College she saw the outlines of the mountains that lay beyond the town. She had often hiked in those mountains with her family. Now she wondered who—or what—had walked there before her. What would she see if she could go back a thousand years? Ten thousand years? A million years? What would the land look like?

She began to daydream, imagining the people who had lived in what was now Beecher Falls. She knew that several American Indian tribes had lived in the area, but that had been fairly recently. What had the earliest inhabitants been like? Recently she had been reading a book about primitive peoples and their ideas of religion, particularly about how the Goddess had been a central figure in many civilizations, even when the people didn't necessarily have a word to describe her. Kate wondered if the inhabitants of her area had worshipped any kind of goddess. Had they made shrines to her out of rocks or other natural materials? Had they drawn pictures of her with chalk and other pigments on cave walls, as many early peoples had?

Kate had never really thought about the history of the land she lived on. Now that she did, she found herself creating images of a girl her age, a girl who lived in the forests thousands of years ago. What would her life have been like? Without things like television and cars and grocery stores—or even real houses or clothes—how would she have seen the world? Would she know that there was anything else besides the forests she lived in? Would she understand what the stars were, or what made the moon get bigger and smaller?

Kate knew from her Wicca studies that the earliest stories about gods and goddesses had been made up to explain natural phenomena like rain and earthquakes and volcanic eruptions. Would the girl she imagined have been told such stories? Would she have believed them? Hearing such stories now,

Kate could appreciate them as legends. But what if she had been alive when they were first told? Would she really have believed in a goddess whose tears made the rain, or whose dancing caused the winds to blow? And as she learned that those things *weren't* caused by supernatural beings, that they were just natural occurrences, would she stop believing in the Goddess?

Isn't that what really did happen? she asked herself. *Didn't people stop believing in the gods and goddesses as they found out more about how the world worked? Didn't they become simply stories that people told, laughing at how silly their ancestors were to believe such things? Isn't that why they were considered myths and legends, and not facts?*

This was something Kate had thought a lot about during her year of studying Wicca. What exactly was the Goddess to her? Did she exist, or was she just a story? Was she simply the personification of nature, or was she something that existed herself? When Kate invited the Goddess into a circle with her, what was she really doing? If someone asked her if the Goddess was real, what would she say? She had once told her brother, Kyle, that she thought of the Goddess as a sort of beehive, a huge entity that was made up of all these other little entities—the bees, or in this case the goddesses who were invoked in magic.

But that didn't answer the question of whether or not she actually *believed* in the Goddess. It was pretty easy for Kate to describe her; it was something else to say whether or not she believed the Goddess existed somewhere. So far it hadn't really been a problem. No one had asked her flat out about her views of the Goddess. But it was something she herself thought about more and more as the time for initiation grew closer.

When she had been confirmed in the church she'd grown up in, as a very little girl, she'd been asked several questions about God and his role in her life. Then it had seemed easy to her to believe in God. She saw him as this old man who lived somewhere in the sky, looking down on the world. Every night when she went to sleep she asked God to look after her and her family, and she'd really believed that he was doing it. She'd believed that when she prayed, God heard her.

Now things didn't seem so simple. She wished she *could* just believe that the Goddess—like the vision of God she'd had as a child—was an old woman who sat up in the clouds and watched what was happening down on Earth. But she knew it wasn't as easy as that. It was difficult for her to put into words exactly how she saw the Goddess, and she didn't know if it was because how she saw the Goddess was difficult to describe, or if it was because she really didn't know what she believed. She very much liked the idea of the Goddess existing in physical form, the way she always did in stories. She liked thinking that maybe she could meet the Goddess in person someday. She'd had several very vivid visions of her before, but what would it be like to actually see her or touch her?

That would make it so much easier to know what I believe, she thought, sighing. Was it this hard for other people? she wondered. Did Sophia and Archer and Thea have these kinds of thoughts? She sometimes wanted to ask them, but she was embarrassed. Everyone else seemed so sure, so confident. She felt like she should be the same way.

"Here." Sherrie dropped a stack of books on the table beside Kate. Annoyed at having her thoughts disturbed, Kate looked at the books.

"Sherrie, these are atlases," she said. "We need books about the physical geography of this part of the country."

Sherrie rolled her eyes and sighed dramatically. "How am I supposed to know what to look for?" she asked. "You can't expect me to do *everything*."

Kate stood up and gathered the books together. Her thoughts about the Goddess were going to have to wait. Right now she had to get to work on her science project. "Come on," she said to Sherrie. "I'll show you where to look."

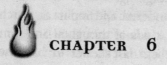

CHAPTER 6

"I can't believe people are up this early," Cooper said sleepily as she stumbled into the kitchen of Juliet's house. She was looking out the window, which overlooked the street. There were people everywhere, walking along and talking. It was just after six in the morning.

Darcy, who was making coffee, laughed. "They aren't up early," she said. "They never went to sleep."

Cooper sat down at the table. Annie was already there, sipping a mug of tea and eating toast with jam on it. She was just as sleepy as Cooper was, but Juliet had told them that they should get up early because she had a big day planned. Since they had stayed up late the night before, waking up had not been easy. Dinner—at a small restaurant serving gumbo and other traditional New Orleans food—had been amazing. Even better had been the conversation. Annie and Juliet had talked about all kinds of things, asking each other questions and comparing stories. They'd continued the conversation back at the house, reluctantly going to bed only when Annie could barely keep her eyes open any longer. Annie hadn't even gotten a chance to give Juliet the gifts she'd brought her.

"Put that down!" Juliet appeared in the kitchen doorway, pointing at Annie and scowling. Annie looked at the piece of toast in her hand, then at Juliet.

"What?" she said. "Is this the last piece of toast or something? I'm sorry."

"No," Juliet said, laughing. "It's just that I have something *much* better in store for you guys. Are you ready to head out?"

"Sure," replied Annie, nodding. "Cooper?"

Cooper, who was resting her weary head on her hand, lifted one hand limply and waved.

"She's ready," Annie told Juliet. "She's not exactly a morning person."

"Let's go, then," said Juliet.

The three of them got up and left the house. As they walked through the streets, Annie tried to take in everything. The city had a totally different look in the morning light than it did at night. While in the evening it blazed with lights and pulsed with energy, in the morning it was like a sleepy child waking up from a nap. The sun dappled the brick buildings with soft, buttery light, and the air was cool. While most of the shops were closed, the little restaurants and cafés were filled with people sitting at tables reading newspapers, drinking coffee, or just enjoying the beauty of the morning.

They emerged into a square. There they saw people setting up all kinds of booths and stalls. Some were arranging paintings against the wrought-iron fences that ran along parts of the square. Others were putting up card tables and hanging signs that said TAROT CARDS READ or FORTUNES TOLD. They passed people setting out jewelry on blankets and jars of hot sauce on tables. It seemed that everyone had something to sell. One stall contained nothing but strings of brightly colored beads.

"I see those beads everywhere," remarked Annie as they passed by. "Everybody seems to be wearing them. Do they mean something?"

"They're Mardi Gras beads," Juliet explained. "It's traditional to give beads to people as gifts. People collect them all during Mardi Gras, but particularly during the parade. You'll see."

She led them across the square, navigating through the people gathering there. "That's where we're going," she said, pointing to a building at the far side of the square. A line of people stretched along the street outside of it. They crossed the street and joined them.

"This is Café Du Monde," Juliet told the girls. "It's probably the most famous coffee shop in the world."

"It must be good if all these people are lined up this early," Annie said.

Juliet nodded. "You're in for a real New Orleans

treat," she said as the line moved forward. "Look at that."

Annie and Cooper looked where Juliet was pointing. A man had emerged from the café holding a bag in one hand and a cup in the other. He opened the bag and pulled out what looked sort of like a square doughnut. It was covered in powdered sugar. He took a bite of it and then sipped from the cup.

"Doughnuts?" Cooper said. "They're famous for doughnuts?"

"Not doughnuts," said Juliet reprovingly. "Beignets. Wait until you try one."

The line had entered the shop and they stopped at a counter. Behind the counter were lots of people removing the beignets from the frying vats and rolling them in tubs of powdered sugar. Juliet placed the order, and moments later they left with three bags and three cups. They sat down on a bench in the square and began to eat.

"This is amazing," said Annie after taking her first bite of beignet. The dough was crispy and soft at the same time, and the sugar melted in her mouth.

"It is *so* not a doughnut," Cooper said approvingly as she tried hers. "It's heaven."

"I told you," said Juliet, licking powdered sugar from her fingers. "Now try the coffee."

Annie and Cooper sipped at their cups, then looked at one another.

"And I thought a Starbucks frappuccino was the perfect drink," remarked Cooper.

Juliet laughed. "Nothing beats the coffee from Café Du Monde," she said. "That place was started in 1862. It's been a fixture of the French Market ever since."

"If I lived here I'd gain fifty pounds the first month just from these," said Annie, starting on her second beignet.

"I almost did," Juliet told her. "Now I only have them on special occasions."

They sat and ate quietly, watching the people come and go around them. Annie was happier than she'd been in a long time. Being in New Orleans felt like being in a place out of time. It was so different from anywhere else she'd ever been. Plus, she was there with Juliet, and that made it even more special.

"Okay," Juliet said when they'd all finished. "Now for the fun."

"You mean it gets better?" asked Cooper as she looked sadly at her empty bag.

"Much better," answered Juliet. "Let's go."

Once more they started walking. This time Juliet led them away from the busy market and down less-crowded streets. They came to a nondescript building, where she opened a door and ushered them inside. "Welcome to the home of the voodoo queen," she said mysteriously as they went through.

They were in what seemed like a big warehouse. Sitting in the middle of the room was a float. The centerpiece was a woman's head, which rose up from the rear of the float. It was made of chicken wire covered with papier-mâché. The head was only half covered, and at the moment four people were busily applying the strips of paper soaked in a mixture of glue and water to the unfinished half, while two others—a woman and a man—painted the finished side. They were applying color to the head's cheeks as Cooper and Annie walked up with Juliet.

"Not bad," Juliet said to the pair doing the painting.

The man stood back and looked at the color, which looked like milky coffee. He was tall and thin, with long light brown hair that was tied into a ponytail in back. He had a short beard and wore round gold-rimmed glasses. He was wearing paint-spattered overalls and a light blue T-shirt. "Do you think Marie would approve?" he asked.

"Definitely," said Juliet. "Now get down here. I want you to meet my sister."

The man jumped down and gave Juliet a kiss. Then he turned to Annie.

"And you must be the famous Annie," he said, bowing solemnly.

Annie laughed. "I guess I am," she said.

The man shook her hand. "I'm Andre," he said. "Juliet has done nothing but talk about you for weeks." He leaned in and said confidentially, "Just between you and me, it's *very* tiresome."

Juliet pretended to be horrified. "Just for that, I'm not helping you with this thing," she said. "You can make the costumes yourself."

Andre grimaced. "That would be ugly," he said. "You know I can't even make curtains."

Juliet turned to the girls. "Andre is my boyfriend," she said. "And he's right, he can't make costumes. But he's an amazing sculptor."

"And actor," Andre said to her. "Don't forget actor."

"And actor," Juliet added, rolling her eyes. "Andre is part of the theater group."

"Part?" said Andre. "I am the *star*."

"Please," Juliet said. "You have how many lines in the latest performance? Six?"

"You're a cruel woman," said Andre. "But now tell me—what do you all think of the float?"

"What is it supposed to be?" Annie asked.

Andre looked at her, narrowing his eyes. "You really *are* her sister, aren't you?" he said. "What is it supposed to be indeed. That," he said, pointing to the head, "is none other than Marie Laveau herself. The rest of it will be done in black and blue and silver. We're going to have people dressed in costumes on the float, throwing out silver beads. It's supposed to capture the essence of voodoo."

"Very spooky," commented Cooper. "This Laveau chick was really something else, huh?"

Andre looked at Juliet. "Perhaps it's time for the tour?" he asked.

"That's what I was thinking," said Juliet. "I have to get busy on those costumes. Do you think you can show them around while I do that, or is your presence here totally indispensable?"

"I think the minions can manage without me," said Andre. He looked at the people working on the float. "Minions?" he called out. "Can you carry on without me for a while?"

The people on the float groaned and waved him away. Andre looked at the girls. "I think they'll be fine," he said.

The four of them walked to the door. Back on the street, Juliet said good-bye and, after arranging to meet them all for lunch later, walked back toward the house. Andre took the girls in the other direction.

"I hope you two aren't easily spooked," he said as they walked. "New Orleans is a peculiar place, and a lot of strange things have happened here over the years. Some people say that there are more ghosts and spirits here than anywhere else on earth."

"I think we'll be okay," said Cooper, giving Annie a knowing look behind Andre's back.

"Well, this morning is all about Marie Laveau and voodoo," Andre said, oblivious to the girls' amusement. "There are so many stories about Marie that it's impossible to know what's true and what isn't. But what is generally accepted as fact is that she was born in 1794, either in New Orleans or perhaps in Haiti. At any rate, she ended up here, where she was a hairdresser. She was famous for organizing dances, which many people believe were just covers for her real ceremonies—the voodoo rituals. You know what voodoo is, right?"

"We have a pretty good idea," Annie told him, not adding that she and Cooper both knew a little about the religion. Also, they had some personal experience with the related religion Santeria, so they understood that basically voodoo was a magical religion based on working with African spirits.

"Okay," Andre said, turning down another street. "Well, Marie Laveau was the queen of voodoo in New Orleans. She held rituals at a small cabin on Bayou Saint John, on the shores of Lake Pontchartrain. There she and her followers danced, sang, and performed magic."

"What kind of magic?" Annie asked. Although she'd read about voodoo rituals, she wondered what exactly people said that Marie Laveau had done.

"Oh, all kinds of things," Andre said. "Marie was supposed to have been able to make people fall in love. She made charms for that, and for good luck. And, of course, she made voodoo dolls."

Again, Annie and Cooper exchanged glances. They'd had their own run-in with a voodoo doll of sorts, and they knew that their powers were not just the stuff of legends. Annie wondered what Marie Laveau had made happen with hers.

Andre stopped and pointed to a gate. "This is where Marie Laveau lived for many years," he said. "The actual house was torn down in the early 1900s, but people still flock here to see the spot. Many claim to see her ghost around here."

Annie and Cooper peered through the gate.

Without an actual house to look at, it was difficult to really get all that excited about a place where something *used* to be. Still, Annie felt a sense of something special about the spot. It had a calmness to it, a sense of reverence that she liked.

"Do you feel her?"

Annie looked up and saw a young woman standing beside her. She was very beautiful, with cocoa-colored skin that was highlighted by the white dress she wore. Her hair was piled on her head and covered by a white scarf. She looked at Annie with dark, alert eyes and smiled.

"You can feel her here, can't you?" she said. "Mam'zelle Marie, I mean. This was her place. Her spirit is here. They can tear down her house, but they cannot get rid of her."

Annie nodded. "Do you know a lot about her?" she asked the young woman.

"This and that," she replied. "I grew up here. Many times I have seen Mam'zelle walking here. She is not to be feared, not by those who pay her their respects, anyway." The girl laughed happily. "Enjoy your stay," she said before turning and walking off.

"Okay," Andre said, bringing Annie's attention back to the moment. "Now it's time for the really cool part."

"Where to?" asked Cooper.

Andre raised his eyebrows. "The cemetery," he said.

Once more they began walking. This time they

walked for quite a while, while Andre told them more about Marie Laveau. "Marie lived for many, many years," he said. "Some say she was well over a hundred. Then one day she walked into her cabin on Bayou Saint John. When she emerged the next morning, she was a young woman again." He looked at the girls. "Then again, some people say the young woman who came out that morning was simply her daughter, Marie II."

They walked until they came to the gates of a cemetery. "Here we are," Andre said. "Saint Louis Cemetery Number One." He led the girls to the gates, where he paused. "According to local superstition, you're supposed to knock three times on the gatepost and ask Saint Peter's permission to enter," he told them. "Otherwise he might not let you out again."

They each knocked three times. Then Andre said, "Shall we?"

He stepped inside, followed by Cooper and then Annie. The cemetery was filled with crypts in various stages of decay. Many of the statues were missing parts, and the tombs themselves were worn away to the point that the names on them were unreadable.

"Because the water table is so high here, they can't bury people in the ground," Andre explained as they walked among the crypts. "Everyone has to be up here. And because of the weather, the stone wears away after a while. But I think this place is beautiful, don't you?"

"Beautiful and creepy," Cooper said. "Where are we going?"

"Right here," Andre announced, stopping before a tall crypt. In front of it there were several white candles in glass containers, along with a scattering of pennies, several bunches of flowers, and a jar of honey. The front of the tomb was covered in small red Xs in groups of three.

"This is where Marie is supposedly buried," Andre said. "Although it may be her daughter who is here and not her. That doesn't matter to most people, though. It's become a shrine. People come from all over to leave offerings here and to ask for Marie's help."

"What's with the Xs?" Cooper asked.

"You leave your offering for Marie," Andre explained. "Then you use one of these to make three Xs," he said, picking up a piece of red brick that was on the ground near the tomb. The girls noticed then that there were numerous pieces of brick there. And judging by the hundreds of rows of Xs, some faded to a ghostly pink and others fresh as blood, many people had stopped by to ask Marie Laveau for help.

"Is there anything you want to ask her for?" Andre asked after they'd looked at the tomb for a few more minutes.

Cooper shook her head. "I'm good," she said.

Annie looked at the Xs, then at the offerings.

"Yes," she said suddenly.

She reached into her pocket and pulled out a handful of change. Selecting three of the shiniest pennies, she laid them at the base of the tomb. Then she picked up a piece of brick and stepped forward. Choosing a fairly clear spot near the top of the crypt's face, she made three neat Xs. Then she stood there, looking at the tomb.

I don't know a lot about you, she thought silently, speaking to Marie Laveau in her mind. *I don't know who or what you really were. But I know magic comes in all forms, and maybe this is just another one of them. Anyway, I want to ask for help with my challenge. I just don't get it. Maybe this is cheating—asking you for help. But I figure I can't be any worse off than I am now. So if you have any ideas, I'd appreciate some help.* She didn't know quite what else to say, so she put the brick down.

"Okay," she said. "I'm done."

Neither Andre nor Cooper asked her what she'd asked for Marie's help with. At the gates they knocked three times again, asked St. Peter's permission to leave, and then exited. As they passed through the gates Annie turned and looked back through the bars at Marie Laveau's tomb. As she did she saw a figure dressed in white standing in front of it. The figure bent down, picked something from the ground, and then appeared to simply vanish. Annie stopped.

"What is it?" asked Cooper.

Annie watched the area around the crypt for a moment. Surely she'd just seen someone doing the same thing she'd done, making an offering to Marie Laveau. The person must have just stepped behind the crypt. That was it.

"Nothing," Annie said. "It was nothing."

But as they walked away, she wondered if she went back to the tomb would her pennies still be there.

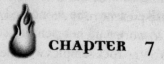

CHAPTER 7

Kate was glad that she'd packed extra socks in her backpack. It was still raining, and beneath the branches of the pine trees there was still snow. Her heavy boots were doing a great job of keeping most of the wetness out, but she knew that she would welcome a change of socks once she got back to the car.

It was Sunday afternoon. She had decided to go on a hike in the mountains outside of town. Since the weather was bad, she knew she would probably be all alone out there. But the area was familiar to her, as she had walked there often, and she knew where she was going. She had talked her parents into letting her use one of the cars for the afternoon, and she had dressed herself in rain gear from her dad's store.

To her surprise, she and Sherrie had actually gotten quite a bit accomplished on Saturday. After Kate had helped Sherrie find the right books, they had located a lot of maps of the area around Beecher Falls showing how the topography had changed over the years. Kate was intrigued to discover that a lot of the area had actually been a rain forest, with towering trees, lots of ferns, and an abundance of water. That accounted for the leaf impressions that were present in the rock samples she and Sherrie had to work with.

Kate carried one of the rock samples with her in her pocket. From time to time as she walked she stuck her hand into her jacket and felt it. It reminded her of why she was there. She wanted to get a feel for the land she lived on. She wanted to really look at it, to imagine being a part of it the way someone living there thousands of years ago might have been a part of it. She knew she couldn't really do that, of course, but she at least wanted to try to capture a little bit of the feeling.

She was walking in a part of the forest that was thick with evergreen trees. While the branches overhead formed a protective canopy, rain still trickled in, dripping from the branches onto her coat and onto her head. Her coat had a hood, but she preferred not to have it up, as she liked being able to feel and smell the air. As a result, her hair was damp, and it clung to her face in tendrils, which she kept brushing away from her cheeks and her eyes as she walked.

The ground beneath the trees was covered in plants. While the rain and the cold prevented them from being as thick as they would be in spring and summer, Kate still felt a little bit like she was in a jungle of sorts. There was no actual trail, and she followed a kind of natural path that wove in between the trees. *But maybe it was a path*, she thought. Maybe there really had been a trail through there at some point, but over the years it had been lost beneath the new layers of pine needles, leaves, and dirt. Maybe she was walking the same path walked by people many, many years ago.

The trail led her up a hill. It was slow going, as the forest floor was more slippery than it usually was. She held on to trees for support as she climbed higher and higher. Twice she had to climb over fallen logs rather than walk the long way around them. By the time she reached the top of the hill she was tired and more than a little wet. She needed a rest.

Walking a little farther, she found that the trees opened up into a small clearing. The pine branches still touched overhead, so the clearing was sheltered from the rain, but there was an open area beneath the trees. The ground there was covered with soft moss, and several stones were situated at one end like a natural bench. Kate went over and sat on them.

Opening her backpack, she took out a thermos of hot chocolate that she'd brought with her. She poured some into the top, which also functioned as a cup, and sipped it. Immediately she felt warmer. She drank half the cup and then set it down on the rock beside her. Then she reached into the backpack again and took out the second of Cooper's presents. She'd almost opened it first thing that morning, but she'd decided to wait until she was in the forest to do it.

Now she pulled the paper off to reveal a flat, wide box. Lifting the lid, she discovered that inside the box was a framed photograph. It was of her, Cooper, and Annie at a ritual. It had been a full moon gathering they'd attended with some members of their class. There had been a bonfire, and the picture showed the three girls standing together in front of the fire. They were wearing white, and they had garlands of white flowers on their heads. Making the photograph even more beautiful was the huge, round moon hanging over their heads.

It was a gorgeous image, and Kate loved it even more because it showed her and her friends taking part in a ritual together. Cooper had put it into a plain wood frame, the simplicity of which set off the photo even more. Kate looked at it and thought of how wonderful that night had been, of how the three of them had really felt like moon goddesses as they'd danced with their friends and celebrated the occasion.

She put the picture back into her backpack so it wouldn't get wet and picked up her cup of hot chocolate again. She sipped it slowly, feeling it move down her throat and into her stomach, warming her up more with each swallow. Her feet weren't as wet as she'd expected them to get, which made her happy. All in all, she was feeling really good. Even having to work with Sherrie wasn't turning out to be as awful as she'd expected it to, and while the disappointment of missing the trip to New Orleans still stung a little, she was okay with it.

She gazed up at the trees towering over her. How old were they? she wondered. She knew that the oldest trees in North America were several thousand years old. The trees she was sitting under weren't nearly that old, but they were pretty old, too. *Too bad you guys can't talk*, she thought as she imagined what kind of stories the trees could tell about what they'd seen. Had explorers walked beneath them once, charting land that no one had ever mapped before? Had native people walked among them? She could only imagine.

She removed the piece of rock from her pocket and looked at it some more. Something else she'd learned in her research was that much of what was now the West Coast of North America had at one time been under the ocean. Some of the rock samples taken from the Beecher Falls area contained remnants of tiny sea creatures, suggesting that where the town lay had not always been dry land. Was the place where Kate was sitting now once part of the ocean floor? Had things like forty-foot prehistoric sharks and enormous fish swum where the trees now grew up to the sky? Thinking about that made her feel a little creeped out, but at the same time it was exciting to imagine that maybe she was sitting where a dinosaur had once walked. Who—or what—would be sitting there two thousand years from now? Would people still live on Earth, or would they be gone, living somewhere in the stars?

A lot of what they studied in their Wicca class had to do with natural cycles. One of the things Kate was finding interesting about her science project was how it, too, was all about cycles. She was investigating the way the natural world she lived in had evolved. Normally the rituals of witchcraft involved shorter cycles, like the changing of the seasons, the waxing and waning of the moon, or even the life and death of a person. The cycles she was learning about now were much vaster than that. It was hard for her to imagine how long a thousand years was, or ten thousand, or a million. But that's how long the Earth had been evolving. And it was still evolving. Someday it would all be different.

Where's my place in all of that? Kate asked herself. *What's my role in the cycle?* That's what her involvement in Wicca was showing her—was supposed to show her. But while she'd learned a lot about herself during the previous months of study and practice, she still sometimes wondered what it all meant, what it was all leading to.

She put the rock away and sat, thinking. Her life had changed so much since she'd gotten involved in Wicca. And it was still changing. Yes, the upcoming initiation ceremony was a big deal. But there was a lot after that as well. There was her senior year, and then college. Then she had her whole life to figure out after that. What did she want to be? What did she want to do?

You can't even figure out the answer to your challenge, she chided herself. *How are you going to figure out your whole life?* She knew she was being hard on herself. But there *were* big decisions she was going to have to make, and soon. Would she be ready for those?

She looked around the clearing again. It was so peaceful there. *It's like a sanctuary,* Kate thought. *Like being in church.* Many times when she was younger and had been worried about something she would go sit in a church. It didn't even matter to her which church it was. Sometimes she would go to St. Mary's, where her family went. Other times she would go to another church, but always one with a big sanctuary where it was quiet. There was a big stone church near her house that she sometimes went to because she loved the soaring ceilings and the old wooden pews with their faded velvet cushions. It smelled of incense and candles and old paper in there, and sitting there surrounded by it all gave her a sense of peace.

That's how she felt now, as if she were sitting in a place where her worries didn't seem quite as pressing, where she could just rest and take time to be quiet. Even the question of her challenge didn't seem like such a big deal there. It was just her and the rain and the forest.

Suddenly she was struck with an idea. Getting up, she walked to the other side of the clearing, where there were some smaller rocks. She piled a few of them up, making a small mound. Then she searched around for some sticks. These she found easily enough. She also found some fern leaves, which she picked. She took these and the sticks back to where she'd been sitting. Looking in the pocket of her backpack, she found some string among the assorted odds and ends she kept in there. She used it to tie the sticks into the shape of a figure. Then she tied some of the fern leaves around what would have been its waist if it had been a real person. The effect was very primitive, but Kate liked it. It reminded her of some kind of ancient drawing.

She took her stick figure and stuck it in the top of the mound of stones so that it stood up by itself. It was supposed to be a forest goddess, and it really did look kind of wild, if a little wet and bedraggled. But Kate didn't care. The whole point had been to create a little shrine to the Goddess, and she'd done that. How long it lasted wasn't important. What was important was that she had made it. Now the clearing felt even more special to her.

She crouched in front of her Goddess image for a while. Then she began to sing, softly. "We all come from the Goddess, and to her we shall return like a drop of rain, flowing to the ocean." It was one of the first chants she'd ever learned, and it was still one of her favorites. It seemed particularly fitting now, as she sat in the clearing with the rain falling.

She really was in the Goddess's house, surrounded by nature, and it felt like home to her.

"Okay," Kate said to the Goddess statue. "Maybe I don't understand my challenge. Maybe I never will. But I've learned a lot from you. So thanks."

She didn't really know what else to say. Really she had just wanted to make the little shrine because it seemed like the right thing to do. Now that it was done, she wondered if she should leave it there or take it down. She decided to leave it. Probably no one else would ever see it because the wind and rain would knock it down, but maybe they would. Maybe someone would decide to hike through there, like she had, and stumble across it while sitting in the clearing for a rest. If they did, would they know what it was? Would they wonder who had made it, and why? Or would they assume it was just a pile of rocks?

Kate liked thinking that someone would see her makeshift shrine. But now it was time for her to leave. She zipped up her pack, slung it onto her back, and, with a final look at the Goddess standing atop the rocks, she left the clearing.

Finding her way back was easy. She walked slowly, savoring her time alone in the woods. When she reached her car again, she slipped off her wet jacket and put it on the floor in the back. Then she removed her boots, put on the extra socks she'd brought, and put her sneakers on over those. Her feet indeed felt toasty, and as soon as she'd started up the car and let the heater run, she was warm again.

When she reached her house her mother's car was gone, meaning she was off at one of her catering gigs. Kate looked at her watch. It was a little after six o'clock. Her father would be closing his store soon. While he could easily take the bus back to the house, Kate decided to surprise him by picking him up. She backed the car out of the driveway and headed into town.

She found a parking spot right in front of the store and squeezed into it. Then she went into the store. Just as she'd thought, her father and the staff were closing up, sweeping the floor and making sure everything was tidied up for the night. Her father was straightening a display of ski equipment, and had his back to her.

"Excuse me," Kate called out in a nasal voice. "I was wondering if you sell lawn furniture?"

"Sure," her father answered. "Right over there behind the riding mowers." He turned around and smiled at Kate. "Don't think you can fool me with a fake voice," he said. "I know all."

"Apparently," Kate said. "So, you want to go to dinner?"

"I think your mother left us stuff in the refrigerator," her father answered.

"I'm sure she did," said Kate. "But I'm sort of in the mood for bad Chinese. What do you say to a little Pooping Panda."

Pooping Panda was what they called Peking

Panda, a Chinese restaurant the family had gone to ever since Kate and Kyle were little kids. Over the years it had gone from being really good to just okay, but they loved the overdone interior, which was all red silk and lanterns, and it still made great hot-and-sour soup, which was what Kate was really in the mood for.

"It's a date," Mr. Morgan said. He turned to one of his assistants. "Rick, I'm leaving with this beautiful young woman. Lock up, and don't tell my wife."

"Sure thing, Mr. M.," Rick replied. "See you tomorrow."

Kate and her father left. Mr. Morgan let Kate drive, and he didn't even correct her once on the way to the restaurant. Soon they were seated in their favorite booth, drinking hot tea and munching on fried wontons dipped in hot mustard sauce.

"So, what's the occasion?" Kate's father asked her.

"What do you mean?" Kate said.

"You never have dinner with your old man," Mr. Morgan said. "Something must be up."

"Nothing's up," Kate replied. "And you're not *that* old."

"Gee, thanks," her father said.

"No," Kate said. "I just thought it would be fun."

Her father eyed her suspiciously but didn't say anything. Kate ate a few more wontons, then said, "Actually, there *is* something I want to talk to you about."

"Ah-ha," said her father, gloating.

Kate hesitated before continuing. "You know I've been taking the Wicca class," she said.

Her father nodded but didn't say anything.

"Well, it's almost over," Kate continued. "It's been almost a year."

She was interrupted by the waiter bringing their food. She waited until he had set down the hot-and-sour soup, followed by the steaming bowl of rice and plates of orange chicken and shrimp with cashews. As she scooped some rice onto her plate she said, "We have to decide now if we want to be initiated or not." She paused before adding, "As witches."

Her father looked at her, a forkful of orange chicken on its way to his mouth. Kate pretended to be very interested in the soup so that she wouldn't have to see the expression on his face.

Mr. Morgan put the chicken into his mouth and chewed. He didn't say anything for a minute, which worried Kate. Usually whenever her father took time to think about something before answering it meant that he was trying to decide how to give bad news.

"And do you?" he said finally.

Kate was shocked. Of all the responses, that was the last one she'd expected.

"I think so," she said before she could over-analyze her father's reaction. "I mean yes, I do want to."

Mr. Morgan took another bite of food, then a sip of his water. Then he looked at Kate, who now was able to look back.

"You know how I feel about this stuff," he said.

Yes, Kate knew. She knew her father thought Wicca was ridiculous. He had been furious when he'd found out she was studying witchcraft. He'd even insisted she see a therapist because of it. They hadn't really spoken about her interest in the Craft since then, although he'd agreed to allow her to keep attending class.

Kate wasn't sure what to say. Was her father telling her that he didn't want her to undergo initiation? One of the conditions of being allowed to go through with the ceremony was the approval of her parents. Sophia had made that very clear to her, especially given the Morgans' initial response to their daughter's involvement in the study group. Even though Kate didn't know yet if she was going to be invited to be initiated, she wanted to talk to her parents about it and sound them out on the subject. If they flat out said no, it would at least make figuring out her challenge easier. But she didn't want them to say no.

"Do you not want me to do it?" Kate asked finally. She figured she might as well get it over with.

"No, I don't want you to do it," her father answered, making the food in her mouth suddenly taste like cardboard. "But I'm not going to stop you," he added a moment later.

"You're not?" said Kate, shocked.

Her father shook his head. "No," he said. "I'm

not. But under one condition."

"Sure," Kate said, ready to agree to anything. "What is it?"

Her father looked at her. "I want you to tell Father Mahoney why you're leaving the church."

"Father Mahoney?" Kate said.

"That's right," said her father. "I want you to sit down with him and talk about this."

"But what does he have to do with anything?" asked Kate. "I'm not his daughter."

"Maybe not," Mr. Morgan said. "But all the same, I want you to talk to him. If you can do that, then you have my permission to do this."

Kate sighed. What kind of game was her father playing with her? She looked at him, but now he was the one busy looking at the food on his plate. He seemed pleased with himself, though. *He's up to something*, Kate thought. She wasn't sure what it was, but she knew her father wouldn't give in so easily if he really thought he was going to lose the fight.

"Okay," Kate said. "I'll talk to him."

"Good," said her father. "I'll give him a call. Now, how about some of this chicken? It's great."

Kate took the plate from him. She was still suspicious. But she was also determined to make it to initiation. If it meant having a talk with Father Mahoney, she could do that. *It just means I have two challenges instead of one*, she told herself as she spooned some chicken onto her plate.

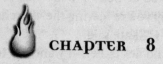

CHAPTER 8

Cooper watched as Juliet hung the painting Annie had brought for her over the fireplace in the living room. Juliet stood on a chair, moving the canvas around, trying to center it.

"Perfect," Annie said as her sister got it exactly right.

Juliet made a mark on the wall with a pencil, then handed the painting down to Annie. She then took a nail and hammered it in with sure strokes. Annie gave her the painting back, and Juliet hooked the wire on the back over the nail. She straightened the painting and turned around.

"How's it look?" she asked Cooper, who was sitting on the couch.

"It's great," answered Cooper.

Juliet climbed down from the chair and put it back in the dining room, where she'd gotten it. Then she returned to the living room and sat down.

"I still can't believe you picked *that* one," Juliet told Annie, who was sitting beside Cooper. "I had a dog who looked just like that when I was a kid. His name was Rabbit."

"Rabbit?" Annie said.

Juliet nodded. "I'd asked for a rabbit," she explained. "Dad brought home a dog instead." She looked at the painting for a minute. "I wish I could have met her," she said. "Both of them." Then she took Annie's hand. "But I'm glad we found each other," she said.

Annie picked up the photo album she'd brought. "Want to see some pictures?" she asked.

"Do you have to ask?" replied Juliet.

Annie opened the photo album and began telling Juliet about the first picture. Cooper listened for a minute and then said, "I'm going to go for a walk."

"I'm sorry," Annie said. "I didn't mean to bore you. It's just that—"

"No," Cooper said, smiling at her friend. "It's not that at all. You guys need some time together, and I'd like to walk around the city. I'll just go out for a while. It's no biggie."

"You're sure?" Annie asked her, sounding concerned.

"I'm sure," Cooper said. "You two have fun. I'll be back around seven."

She left the sisters in the living room and went outside. The afternoon sun was warm, and she was happy to be on her own, walking around New Orleans. She was having a great time with Annie—

and she really liked Juliet and her friends—but she wasn't used to being around people all the time. Being able to walk around by herself made her feel like she was alone. Even though she was surrounded by hundreds of people, none of them were people she had to talk to.

She really didn't have a particular destination in mind. She just wanted to walk around and see what she found. She liked walking around cities she had never been in. Tourist attractions didn't interest her; she was more interested in finding out what the people who lived in the city were like, what their real lives were like.

She headed away from Bourbon Street with its gaudy gift shops and hawkers trying to get people to come into the bars and restaurants. As she moved farther away from the busier tourist areas, she found that the shops she passed changed. Gone were the garish Mardi Gras masks and the endless piles of New Orleans T-shirts. Instead, she was walking by old bookshops and galleries selling work by local artists. The noisy, crowded bars were replaced by quieter neighborhood establishments.

She began to relax. While she enjoyed the energy of the crowds that thronged the area around Bourbon Street, sometimes she preferred things to be quieter. It helped her clear her mind, and she could think about things. All morning she and Annie had helped Juliet, Andre, and the others work on the Mardi Gras float. They'd gotten a lot accomplished, and Cooper had had fun doing some of the painting. It was interesting to see the float come to life, and she was anxious to see the finished product. But right now she was happy to be just walking along in the late-afternoon sun.

As she passed the doorway of a little restaurant she heard music coming from inside. Pausing, she listened. Someone was playing a guitar. But it wasn't the usual random playing that she often heard from people sitting on stoops or in parks. This was real playing. It was old-time blues. And it was great.

She stood outside, listening to the guitarist. One of the things that had gotten her interested in guitar in the first place was hearing old blues records, records by people like John Lee Hooker, B. B. King, and Muddy Waters. The sound was so different from the pop music they played on most radio stations. It had real feeling to it, and she had loved listening to the way the guitar players seemed to be telling stories. The playing she was hearing now reminded her of that kind of music.

"If you're going to stand there, you might as well come on in," said a voice.

Cooper looked up and saw an old woman standing in the doorway. She was wearing a white apron over her blue dress, and she was wiping her hands on a dish towel. Her once-black hair had turned almost pure white, and her dark skin was wrinkled with age. She looked at Cooper with bright eyes and a small smile.

"Thanks," Cooper said, smiling back and stepping inside the restaurant.

It was small, and not much to look at. The wooden floor was covered in sawdust, and there were only a dozen or so little tables, which really weren't more than picnic tables covered with red-and-white-checked tablecloths. Swinging doors on the far side of the room led to what Cooper guessed was the kitchen, and there was a bar along one wall. A few of the tables were occupied by people drinking beer or enjoying bowls of gumbo.

At the front of the restaurant an old man was sitting in a straight-backed chair, a guitar on his lap. He was the one Cooper had heard playing. He sat with his eyes closed, his fingers moving over the strings as his body rocked slowly from side to side.

"Why don't you have a seat over here," the old woman said to Cooper, leading her to a table near the old man.

Cooper sat down. A moment later the old woman came back and set down a big glass of water and a basket of hush puppies. The crispy fried pieces of cornmeal bread were just out of the pan, and they smelled wonderful. Cooper dipped one in the little dish of sauce the old woman gave her and bit into it.

"Good, aren't they?" the woman asked her.

Cooper nodded. "Delicious," she said.

The woman looked at her appraisingly. "I think you need yourself some crawfish," she said.

"Oh, no," Cooper protested. "I'm not really

hungry. This will be fine."

The woman shook her head. "Crawfish," she said. "You just sit right there. I'll be back."

Before Cooper could say anything else, the old woman turned and disappeared through the swinging doors. Cooper sighed. It looked like she was getting crawfish whether she wanted them or not. She really didn't know if she *did* want them. She was a vegetarian, and normally she avoided anything that, as she put it, "had a face." But she sometimes ate shrimp, she told herself, and crawfish weren't much different. Besides, the old woman seemed intent on feeding her, and Cooper didn't want to disappoint her. Plus, Cooper felt like she was on some sort of adventure, and one thing she'd learned during her months of studying Wicca was that she should *never* turn down an adventure.

While she waited for her crawfish, she listened to the man playing the guitar. He hadn't stopped playing yet, and seemed content to keep right on playing the same beautiful music that had drawn Cooper in in the first place. The song made her think of all kinds of seemingly unrelated things: a slow-flowing river, fireflies blinking in the darkness, T.J., standing in a ritual circle holding hands with people on either side of her, listening to the sound of rain on her bedroom roof. It was almost dreamlike, yet there was a harshness to it as well, a sadness, as if the song was supposed to remind the listeners that life was hard but wonderful.

The old woman returned carrying a big white bowl heaped with bright red crawfish. They were still steaming, and the smell rising from them was a combination of salt, garlic, and hot pepper.

"They're boiled in my secret recipe," said the old woman as she set the bowl down in front of Cooper, along with a stack of napkins and little bowls of butter and more hot sauce.

Cooper looked at the crawfish. They were sort of like miniature lobsters. But she wasn't sure how to eat them. The old woman, noticing her hesitation, laughed.

"Like this," she said, picking up a crawfish. First she broke a claw off and, putting it between her teeth, cracked it open and sucked on it. She repeated the process with the other claw, then turned her attention to the crawfish's tail. Holding it in her hands, she gently split it open, peeling away the shell and throwing it into an empty bowl that sat on the table. She pulled the tail meat away from the body and dipped it into the butter before eating it.

"Now for the best part," she said. Taking the crawfish's head, she placed it in her mouth so that the creature's eyes and antenna were hanging out and, to Cooper's horror, sucked on the open end. Then she cast the empty head into the bowl with the rest of the shell.

"Try it," the woman instructed Cooper.

Cooper looked doubtfully at the bowl of craw-fish. She wasn't sure she could do it. *It's part of the adventure*, she told herself. *You have to face your fears.* Face her fears. The idea suddenly struck her as being very funny. Surely crawfish weren't her greatest fear? No, this wasn't her big challenge. But it definitely was some kind of challenge. *And if you can't face this one, how are you going to face the really big ones?* she asked herself.

Here goes nothing, she thought as she picked up a crawfish. Imitating the old woman, she pulled a claw off and put it in her mouth. When she bit down, it split open. She sucked on it a little, and was rewarded with a piece of sweet, tender meat. It was delicious, and she put the second claw into her mouth without hesitation. The tail was even better, especially soaked in butter and dipped in the sauce, which turned out to be a mixture of horseradish and hot pepper.

But the head was something else. When it came time to eat it, Cooper could only stare at the crawfish's beady black eyes. *Why would anyone want to put that in their mouth?* she asked herself.

"You *got* to suck the head."

Cooper looked up and saw the man who had been playing the guitar watching her, along with the old woman. He had an amused but friendly look on his face. "Go on," he said encouragingly. "Suck the head. It's the best part."

Cooper turned the head around and looked inside of it. She could see some yellowish material in the crawfish's cavity. She did not want to eat it.

But the old couple were looking at her. Besides, she had agreed to take the adventure.

Before she could stop herself or think about it anymore, she put the head in her mouth and sucked. Immediately her mouth was filled with something soft, almost like mashed potatoes. It had a salty taste that wasn't at all unpleasant. Cooper swallowed and then darted her tongue into the head. Finding nothing left in there, she put the shell into the bowl.

"That's the way!" the old man said, clapping her on the shoulder. "Don't tell me that was your very first crawfish?"

"My very first," said Cooper, wiping her mouth on a napkin and then picking up another crawfish. Now that she knew what to expect, she found she couldn't wait to have another one.

"Mind if I sit down?" the old man asked her.

Cooper shook her head. "Go right ahead," she said.

He sat and picked a crawfish from the bowl. In a matter of seconds he had sucked the claws clean and eaten the tail. Then he put the head in his mouth and drew out the contents.

"Nothing better than crawfish," he said as he tossed the shell into the bowl. He took another, and looked at Cooper before starting on it. "What brought you in here?" he asked her.

Cooper took the claw she was sucking out of her mouth. "The music," she said. "I was walking by and I heard you playing. It's great."

The man fixed her with an interested look. "Not many your age stop when they hear *this* kind of music," he said. "Not many your sex, either, if you don't mind me saying so."

"I know," Cooper said. "You're wondering why this little white girl loves old blues music."

The old man laughed raucously. "I wasn't going to say anything about the *white* part," he said. "But since you brought it up, yes, that's just what I was wondering."

Cooper added another shell to the rapidly filling bowl. "I just love it," she said. "I don't think I can even tell you why. I just love the sound that guitar makes, especially the way you play it. I wish I could play like that."

"You play?" the man asked her.

Cooper nodded. "Not like that, but I play."

"You want to play like that, you just got to open your heart," said the old man. "You just got to *feel*." He looked closely at Cooper. "Why'd you come here?" he asked. "To New Orleans, I mean."

"I came with a friend," Cooper answered. "Her sister lives here."

The old man nodded. "Uh-huh," he said, almost grunting. He dunked a crawfish tail in the hot sauce. "I think you came here for something else," he said. "I think you came here to find the answer to a question."

Cooper took a drink of water. What the old man said was sort of true. She *had* come to New

Orleans because of Annie, but she had been more than a little preoccupied with finding out what her challenge was all about.

"There is something I've been trying to figure out," she told him.

"Thought so," the man said. "You should ask Sunny about that."

"Sunny?" Cooper repeated.

"Her," the old man said, nodding at the woman who had drawn Cooper into the restaurant. "This is her place."

He waved Sunny over. "This child needs you to help her," he said before Cooper could even say anything. "Maybe you make her a gris-gris."

A what? Cooper wondered. The word the man had said sounded like *gree-gree*. "What's that?" she asked.

"You don't know crawfish. You don't know gris-gris. What *do* you know?" the old man teased. "A gris-gris is a charm. Powerful voodoo magic."

"Oh, it ain't voodoo," Sunny said. "It's just plain old magic. You believe in magic?" she asked Cooper.

"Yes," Cooper said. "As a matter of fact, I do. Very much."

"I thought as much," said Sunny. "What kind of problem are you having?"

Cooper thought about the best way to explain her situation. "I'm supposed to be figuring out a problem," she said vaguely. "Kind of like the answer to a question."

Sunny regarded her for a moment. "Come in back with me," she said.

Cooper stood up and followed Sunny, leaving the old man at the table, happily sucking crawfish heads. Sunny led her through the swinging doors into a small kitchen. Huge pots of water boiled on the stove, and bowls of crawfish—both cooked and still crawling around—stood everywhere. Sunny passed by them and into another, smaller room. This one was lined with shelves containing glass jars filled with what looked like herbs. There were also bunches of dried plants hanging from the ceiling, as well as assorted strange objects sitting on the long table that was pushed against one wall.

Sunny went to the table and opened a drawer. She pulled out a small black cotton drawstring bag. This she pulled open and set on the table. Then she took down several jars, pausing momentarily before selecting each one, until she had five of them on the table.

She opened the first one and took out what looked like a dried root. "A little High John never hurt nobody," she said as she put it into the bag. "And I think some bay leaf and some devil's weed."

She added more things to the bag, including what looked like several green peppercorns and a small nail. Then she opened a small jar and dumped something odd-looking onto the counter—something that looked like it had a lot of legs.

"Is that a spider?" Cooper asked Sunny.

"Used to be," Sunny said, picking the dead spider up and adding it to the bag. "You'll be wanting its weaving powers."

She looked around for a moment then, seeming satisfied, pulled the string on the bag shut. Holding it in her hands, she said some words Cooper couldn't hear. Then she turned and held it out.

"Keep this with you," she told Cooper. "It will help you solve your problem."

Cooper looked at the bag. She was thinking particularly about the dead spider. It all seemed a little creepy to her. But Sunny seemed like a really nice person.

"Take it," said Sunny. "It will work. Trust me. It worked for my mother, and for her mother before her, and her mother before her." She was grinning, and her happiness was infectious. With a smile, Cooper took the bag from her.

"Thank you," she said. She started to reach into her pocket for some money.

"No money," Sunny said, waving her hands. "It is a gift from me to you, a gift for coming into my restaurant and trying my crawfish. Those, though, will be five dollars and ninety-nine cents."

Cooper laughed. She and Sunny returned to the main room, where the old man was polishing off the last of the crawfish.

"Sunny," he said. "Bring us another bowl."

"Oh, I can't," Cooper said. "I have to meet my friends. But thank you." She turned to Sunny.

"Thank you for everything."

"You'll see," the old man said to Cooper. "Sunny's gris-gris will work like no magic you've ever seen. And you remember what I told you about those blues—listen to your heart. If you hear what it's saying, you'll be able to play it."

"Thanks," said Cooper. "I'll try."

She left the restaurant and walked back toward Juliet's house. It had been a strange afternoon—a very strange afternoon. She'd sucked on crawfish heads, listened to some great music, and now she was heading home with a bag containing a dead spider. But somehow it all made sense. There was a reason she'd been drawn to Sunny's restaurant. She didn't know what it was yet, just as she didn't know what her challenge was. But she was getting closer. She could feel it.

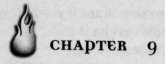

CHAPTER 9

"How are we supposed to know which rock goes where?" asked Sherrie impatiently.

She and Kate were once again in the Jasper College library. This time they had laid out the rock samples—seven in all—on one of the tables. They were attempting to put them in order from the oldest to the most recent.

"This handout tells which one is which," Kate told her. "Look for the igneous one first."

"The ignorant one?" said Sherrie, making a face. "What's *that*?"

"Not ignorant," Kate said. "Igneous. It means a rock formed from fire or volcanic activity. One of the rock samples is from the period when there was a lot of volcanic activity in this area."

"How do I know which one it is?" Sherrie said, her voice whiny.

Kate sighed and silently counted backward from five in her head. It was her latest trick for dealing with Sherrie. When she reached one she said, as patiently as possible, "It's the black one. See how it looks like it's smoother than the others? That's because the fire melted the minerals that it's made of."

Sherrie picked up the rock and looked at it. She ran her fingers over the smooth surface. "Oh," she said, putting it down again. "Whatever."

"Okay," Kate said, looking at the lineup of rocks. "I think we've pretty much got it. Although we might want to switch the sedimentary rock with the metamorphic one."

Sherrie sniffed. "You don't have to show off for me, you know," she said. "I don't care whether or not you know the difference between concrete and Italian marble."

"I'm not showing off for you," Kate answered as she shuffled the rocks around a little. "I happen to think this is interesting."

"Right," Sherrie said. "I guess it's all part of the new Kate, huh? You know, the one who decided her old friends weren't good enough once she got all into the hocus-pocus stuff."

Kate looked at Sherrie with a bewildered expression. "What are you talking about?" she asked.

Sherrie gave a sharp laugh. "Please," she said. "I know all about it. You and your little friends who think you're witches. Everybody knows, Kate, and everybody thinks it's ridiculous."

"Is that so?" Kate asked. "Just what is it that everyone knows, Sherrie?"

Sherrie looked away for a moment, then looked back with a sour expression. "I don't know how you can think any of that stuff is real," she said.

"You don't even have the slightest idea what you're talking about," Kate informed her. "Why don't we just stick to the assignment. That way you can avoid looking like an uninformed idiot."

"First that Rivers freak tries to show up my dad," Sherrie said, clearly not intending to stick to the assignment. "Then that Crandall girl writes that article for the paper. And Alissa Coker said she saw the three of you doing some kind of sacrifice down at the beach one night. She said she heard a cat screaming."

Kate laughed despite herself. "Oh," she said. "I see. Alissa heard us skinning that cat. Next time we'll have to make sure we do it in a basement."

She watched Sherrie's expression turn from one of condescension to one of disgust. Then she rolled her eyes. "Witches don't sacrifice animals," she said. "Or people," she added when she saw Sherrie start to say something. "If Alissa Coker saw anything, it was us doing a full moon ritual. And if she heard anything making noise, it was probably a seagull. They sound a lot like cats."

"So you *were* doing something," said Sherrie, as if she'd won a major point in the argument.

"Yes, we do rituals," Kate said. She hadn't intended to get into the subject with Sherrie, but now that she had she figured she'd set the record straight. "And yes, we go to a Wiccan study group. But we aren't witches. Not yet."

"What?" Sherie said. "You're waiting for your brooms to arrive?"

"Yeah," Kate said, tiring of the conversation. "And our hats. You can't graduate without the hat."

She returned to looking at the rocks. Now that she had the samples pretty much dated, it was time to link them to particular types of geologic activity. She had begun to sketch out a timeline for the changes that had taken place in the surrounding area, beginning with the time when the forests around Beecher Falls were just beginning to grow.

"No, really," Sherrie said. "What makes someone a real witch instead of just a pretend one—you know, what you and your freaky friends are."

Kate counted backward again, this time from ten. When she reached the beginning she still wasn't as calm as she wanted to be, and her voice carried more than a hint of irritation when she said, "I really don't think this is any of your business."

"Fine," Sherrie said. "I'm just trying to understand it is all."

Kate almost laughed. Sherrie trying to understand something about someone else was like a terrorist claiming he always checked to make sure there were no kittens inside a building before blowing it up. It just wasn't plausible. Kate's first instinct was to just ignore her and get back to work. But she knew Sherrie would consider even that

117

reaction a victory. She would think that Kate was admitting that Wicca really *wasn't* something legitimate. And that made Kate mad.

"Okay," she said, setting down the metamorphic rock. "Do you really want to know what makes someone a witch?" She didn't wait for Sherrie's answer before continuing. "A witch is someone who has dedicated her life to learning about the connections between things. She studies the different cycles and her place in them. She learns how to use the energy in herself and in the world to make changes. And most of all, she tries to make the world a better place for herself and other people."

She stopped. She'd never put her views about being a witch into such a concise form. In fact, she wasn't even sure where the words had come from. She certainly had never organized her thoughts like that. But listening to herself speak, it was as if she was reciting a rehearsed speech.

"Make the world a better place?" said Sherrie sarcastically. "I suppose that's what you all were doing when Annie pushed Terri Fletcher down the stairs, or when Cooper demanded to be able to wear her stupid necklace to school, even though it bothers a lot of people."

"Annie never pushed Terri," retorted Kate. "And yes, Cooper made things better by standing up for her beliefs. Just because you don't agree with them—or with what she did—that doesn't mean there's anything wrong with being a witch."

"I think you're all just trying to be different," Sherrie said, as if explaining something to a small child. "You just want to shock people."

Right, Kate thought. *I spent five months in therapy because I wanted to shock people. We all got attacked by those college guys because we wanted to shock people. This is all just us having a lot of fun.* But she didn't say any of that. What she said was, "Like I said, you don't have to understand it. None of us are doing this for your benefit."

She turned her attention back to the rocks. She opened a reference book and started to look up information about the effects of volcanic activity on the vegetation of a region. Sherrie watched her for a minute, not saying anything. Then she said, "I feel sorry for you, Kate. You used to be popular. Now look at you. You're hanging out with losers and getting into rocks. I wouldn't want to be you for anything in the world."

Kate's blood was boiling. She wanted more than anything to give Sherrie a piece of her mind. She wanted to tell her that *she* was the loser, that *she* was the one everyone felt sorry for—that is, when they weren't busy wishing she'd fall off a cliff or choke on a chicken bone. How dare Sherrie think for one minute that *Kate* was the one who should be pitied, when everyone knew that Sherrie Adams was the saddest, the most pathetic, the most *obnoxious* girl in all of Beecher Falls and possibly in the world?

All of these things raced through Kate's mind as she pretended to be studying the book in front of her. All of these things and more. She was just trying to decide which of them to begin with. By the time she was done with Sherrie, Sherrie would be sorry she had ever even brought up the subject of Kate's involvement in Wicca.

But then, just before she opened her mouth to begin her full frontal assault on Sherrie, something came over Kate. It was a sense of calm, the feeling that everything was okay. She didn't need to explain herself to Sherrie. Sherrie didn't matter. What mattered was how she herself felt. Sherrie could think whatever she wanted to.

"I have to go look for another book," Kate said, completely ignoring Sherrie's remark. "Why don't you see if you can find something about how old the forests are around here?"

She turned and left, not waiting for Sherrie to answer. She knew Sherrie would be annoyed by the fact that Kate had let her remark go by without getting upset about it. Everything Sherrie said was designed to make people unhappy, and by not letting her comments get to her, Kate had succeeded in doing exactly what Sherrie didn't want. That was even better, she thought, than if she'd come up with some witty retort.

She really didn't have another book to look for. She just wanted to get away from Sherrie. So she spent a few minutes looking through the shelves and then returned to the table. To her surprise, Sherrie was looking at the book and writing something down. *She's doing work*, Kate thought as she approached. *I might die of shock.*

"I was just writing you a note," Sherrie said when Kate arrived at the table. "I have something to do, so I'm leaving."

"Oh," said Kate. *Of course she wasn't doing any work*, she thought. *She was just trying to make a getaway.*

Sherrie collected her coat and her backpack. "'Bye," she said. That was it. No explanation of where she was going. No offer to do any of the work. No anything. Just "'Bye."

Kate watched her go. It was just as well. She could work faster—and better—on her own. At this point, she didn't even care if Sherrie so much as helped carry a book from the shelf to the table. She sat down and got back to work. Picking up the first rock sample, she began to write a paragraph about it and about the conditions under which it was most likely formed.

She worked for about an hour, then decided that she'd done enough. They—or rather she—was way ahead on the assignment. At the rate she was going, she would be done well before the three-week deadline. *I could have gone to New Orleans and still gotten this done,* she thought a little sadly. But she pushed that thought from her mind. There was no point in dwelling on it. Besides, she was going to hang out with Sasha that evening, and she was looking forward to that.

She gathered up her stuff, returned the reference books to the shelves, and left the library. It had stopped raining, but now everything was a frozen, gray mess. The world looked washed-out and tired, and it made her feel tired as well. She longed for bright sunshine and warm winds. The Spring Equinox was approaching, and she couldn't wait. Besides marking the arrival of spring, the ritual would be the first one she, Annie, and Cooper were helping to organize. They'd been discussing ideas for weeks, and pretty soon they would get started on their ideas.

It was hard for her to believe that their dedication ceremony had been almost a year ago already. It seemed like only days since she, Cooper, and Annie had attended that first Ostara ritual. And in fact, Kate had almost not shown up at all. She'd been doubting her involvement in Wicca and had been very close to skipping out on the ritual. But at the last minute she'd gone, and she'd had a good time.

Not only was it her first ritual with real witches, it was where she had met Sasha. Thinking about that made her laugh to herself. Her first impressions of Sasha had not been good ones—probably because Sasha had been wearing the robe Kate had sewn for herself. Sasha had been a much different person then, a frightened runaway hiding behind a lot of bravado. But luckily Kate and her friends had seen through it and given her a second chance. *And a third, fourth, and fifth chance*, Kate thought, remembering how difficult it had been to get Sasha to trust them, and for them to trust her.

That had also been the ritual where Kate had met Tyler for the first time. Thinking about that made her a little sad. Things with him had not ended the way she would have liked, even if they had ended for the best. *It's just another cycle*, Kate reminded herself as she thought about how she and Tyler had gone from being totally into one another to being forced apart by her parents to breaking up after he'd fooled around with Annie. Getting over that had been difficult for Kate, but she'd learned a great deal about herself since that first ritual, and she'd been able to put everything behind her. Things with Annie were back to normal, although Kate didn't really talk to Tyler much. He'd tried to get back together with her, and when she'd said no he had pretty much stopped talking to her. Not that they saw each other often.

But we would if I join the Coven of the Green Wood, Kate thought. That was one aspect of initiation she hadn't even allowed herself to think about yet. If they passed their challenges and were offered initiation, they would be expected to choose a coven to join. That pretty much meant either the Coven of the Green Wood, of which Tyler and his mother were a part, or the coven that ran Crones' Circle. Thinking about that, Kate realized for the first time that she didn't even know the name of the coven to which Sophia, Archer, and the others belonged. Whatever it was, it would be one of her choices.

She loved the rituals she'd gone to that were organized by the Coven of the Green Wood. She liked a lot of the people in it. But could she really belong to a coven with her ex-boyfriend? That was just a little too weird. *It's like a really bad Jerry Springer episode*, she thought. And even if she did join Sophia's and Archer's coven, the two covens frequently worked together, which meant she would be doing circles and rituals with Tyler anyway.

She sighed. Nothing could be easy, could it? And this was all assuming that she was offered initiation in the first place. That was far from guaranteed. Cooper and Annie were shoo-ins, she knew, but she was a different story. She'd always been the one of the three of them who seemed the least likely candidate for witchdom. Over the past months she'd become much more comfortable with Wicca, and with being a part of it. Still, she knew she wasn't classic witch material. Maybe the people deciding their fates would think she wasn't ready. Maybe they would tell her she could still come to public rituals but not be a full coven member. What would she do then? Would she be able to stand seeing Annie and Cooper doing things with whichever covens they joined and knowing they were part of something she could only observe from the outside? In many ways that would put her right back to where she was when she'd started studying Wicca, and she didn't think it was something she'd be able to do. She would probably have to stop practicing Wicca altogether. As for her friendship with Cooper and Annie, well, the incident with Tyler and Annie had shown her that nothing could destroy that. Still, it would be changed.

Of course, none of this would even matter if she didn't get to work on solving her challenge. The question with no answer still had not come to her, even though she'd thought about it a lot. She'd been reading all kinds of fairy tales, looking for clues, and while they'd been interesting, none of them had been particularly helpful, at least not unless she'd been asked what it was that Bluebeard kept in his forbidden room (heads), how to distract an angry dwarf (tell it to count the straws in a haystack), or how to keep a selkie from turning from a woman back into a seal (hide its seal skin). But these questions, she was fairly certain, were not going to be on the final exam, so to speak. No, she had to try something else.

She reached her house and let herself in. No one was home, but when she went into the kitchen she saw the message light on the answering machine blinking. She hit play and listened as the machine played back the messages.

"Hey, kids. It's Netty. Just calling to see what everyone is up to. I'm flying to Switzerland on Wednesday to shoot some ski thing, so call me before then. 'Bye. Oh, and blessed be."

Kate laughed. She was glad to hear her aunt sounding so happy. Since her cancer had gone into remission, she'd gotten back to her job as a photographer, and she was enjoying it more than ever. Because of her experiences with some Wiccan healing circles during her illness, she'd also gotten more and more into Wiccan spirituality, which thrilled Kate. Hearing her aunt's "blessed be" greeting made her feel like they shared even more than they had before Netty's diagnosis.

The second message also caught Kate's attention, but for a different reason. "Hello, Joe, this is Father Mahoney over at Saint Mary's. I'd be happy to speak with Kate. How about tomorrow afternoon, say around three. Have her come over to my office."

The message ended and the machine clicked off. Kate stared at it for a moment. She'd sort of forgotten about her promise to her father. But he clearly hadn't. She wondered what he'd told Father

Mahoney about why Kate needed to talk to him. It wasn't as if he didn't already know about her interest in witchcraft. After all, it had been his idea that she see a therapist in the first place. He and Dr. Hagen were friends, and while Kate had really enjoyed her sessions with the doctor, she wasn't sure she was going to enjoy her conversation with Father Mahoney.

She took her backpack upstairs, feeling slightly dejected. When she set it down, she saw Cooper's gift box and realized that she hadn't opened the day's present yet. She took out number 3 and felt it. It was an odd shape, and she really couldn't guess what it might be. *There's one way to find out*, she thought as she opened it.

It turned out to be a bottle of bubble solution. Kate unscrewed the top and pulled out the little plastic wand inside. Dipping it into the sudsy water, she blew through it, sending dozens of tiny bubbles cascading into the air. Watching them lifted her spirits a little. It was a silly thing, but it was fun.

She blew more bubbles—this time bigger ones. As each one separated from the wand and floated away, it felt as if one of her worries was leaving her. She blew more and more, sending new ones out before the old ones could burst. Soon she was surrounded by bubbles. She watched them swirling around, and she felt herself cheer up considerably.

Everything would be fine. She would finish her challenge. She would talk to Father Mahoney, as her father had asked. It would all be okay.

"Thanks, Cooper," she said, thinking of her friends and hoping they were having a good time. "I needed that."

CHAPTER 10

A sea of faces. That's what Annie saw. There were people *everywhere*. They were crowding the streets. They were standing on balconies. They were pouring out of the bars and restaurants. She'd never seen so many people in one place in her life. And they were all having a great time. They were dancing and laughing and cheering. Most of them had several strands of brightly colored beads around their necks, and they were calling out for more.

A man whose face was painted in purple and gold swirls waved at her. His bare chest was adorned with numerous strands of beads already, but he clearly wanted even more. Annie tossed him some silver beads and he caught them, cheering and swinging them over his head before putting them around his neck. He blew Annie a kiss, and she laughed.

Mardi Gras was unbelievable. The air was practically crackling with the energy being raised by all the partying people. From her vantage point on top of the float, Annie could see over their heads, and to her it seemed like the very air was shimmering with joy. She had been thrilled when Andre and Juliet told her that she and Cooper could ride on the float if they wanted to. "It's really the best way to see the parade without being overwhelmed by all the people," Andre had told them.

The two girls had readily agreed. All that was required of them was that they dress up in costumes made of shiny blue, silver, and black material. Their faces had been painted as well, so that they resembled some weird kind of clowns. Voodoo clowns, Cooper had dubbed them, and she wasn't far off.

The float itself was gorgeous. The krewe had done an amazing job over the final few days, transforming the bare-bones float into something spectacular. The papier-mâché Marie Laveau looked very real indeed now that she was painted and costumed. She loomed behind Annie and the others, her arms held up to the moon, which was almost full, so that it looked as if Marie were playing catch with it. A costumed dancer stood on each upraised hand, both dancers dressed in simple white dresses and head coverings.

The rest of the float looked like a Louisiana bayou, with giant, dreamlike flowers and lots of blue material arranged to look like water. Both the flowers and the water rustled in the wind, and the whole float looked alive. Annie, Cooper, and the others were supposed to represent the spirits of the bayou, called forth by Marie's magic. They each had baskets of silver bead necklaces at their feet, and they tossed these necklaces out to the crowd as the float moved down the street.

"This is insane," Cooper said to Annie. "It's like being at a rock concert or something."

"I know," Annie said. "I just hope we don't run out of beads. How much farther do you think we have to go?"

Cooper looked down the street ahead of them. There were a lot of floats in the parade, and they were about seventh in line.

"I can't tell," Cooper told her. "They turn a corner up there."

As they continued to rumble along, throwing beads to the onlookers, Annie thought about the past few days. She and Juliet had had several long talks, and Annie felt as if they were really getting to know each other. It still felt strange, having a big sister. She had always been the oldest. She was the one Meg came to with her problems and her questions. Now Annie had someone to do that with, if she wanted to. She'd always had her Aunt Sarah, but that was different. She wasn't sure exactly *how* it was different, but it was. An aunt was one thing, but a sister was another.

And pretty soon you'll have another sister, she thought. Becka. As soon as Aunt Sarah and Grayson Dunning got married and he and Becka moved in with them, she would have yet another sister in her life. The tight little trio of herself, Meg, and Aunt

Sarah was expanding rapidly, opening up to include all kinds of people. Annie liked that. It made her think of being part of a coven, where people of all kinds came together to work magic together. That was a kind of family as well.

She still hadn't discussed the whole Wicca thing with Juliet. She was fairly sure her sister wouldn't be too weirded out by it—especially given some of the stuff Annie had seen in New Orleans—but she wasn't quite ready to come out of the broom closet to her.

Something landed at her feet, distracting her. She looked down and saw several shiny silver dimes scattered on the truck bed. She looked out into the crowd. There she saw a little girl wearing a Mardi Gras mask made of white feathers and dressed all in white. She was looking up at the giant head of Marie Laveau, and she seemed lost in wonder.

It wasn't the first time coins had been tossed onto the float. On several occasions Annie had seen people throw handfuls of coins—always silver—onto the passing truck. Always they stared in reverence at the papier-mâché head. It was as if they were paying their respects to Marie Laveau. And always, after presenting their offerings, the people disappeared quietly into the crowd, as if they had come just to see the voodoo queen pass by.

Coins. Annie's train of thought brought her, neatly but not happily, to the subject of her challenge. She'd successfully avoided thinking about it for the past couple of days. She'd been so busy sightseeing and helping with the float that she'd been able to push it to the back of her mind. Once or twice she'd thought about her visit to St. Louis Cemetery Number 1, and the pennies she'd left for Marie Laveau, but she'd never allowed herself to dwell on it for too long.

The truth was, she was no closer to figuring out what her most precious possession was than she had been at the moment when she'd chosen her slip of paper from the Challenge Box. She was pretty certain that she knew what it *wasn't*, and that was something, but she couldn't stop there. She had to solve the puzzle and come up with the correct answer, otherwise she would fail. *And you cannot fail this challenge*, she reminded herself sternly.

She and Cooper had managed not to talk about the challenges at all, which both pleased and frustrated Annie. She was used to sharing things with her friends. They often helped her figure out problems she was having, and together they had come up with all kinds of great magical ideas. Now that they were on their own, it made Annie see even more clearly just how important it was to her to have a web of friends she could talk with and work magic with. While she realized that walking the Wiccan path was ultimately something that each witch did alone, her work during the past year had shown her time and time again that working with others taught her a lot and made it all much more fun.

She knew that something had happened to Cooper on Sunday. Her friend had returned to the house in a surprisingly upbeat mood for her, and she'd worn a secretive smile for the rest of the evening. But try as she might, all Annie could get out of Cooper was that she'd gone somewhere to listen to music and learn how to eat crawfish. She'd even proven it to Annie by teaching her how to suck crawfish heads, impressing Juliet, Andre, and Darcy, who had joined them for supper.

What had happened to Cooper? she wondered. And why wasn't anything happening for *her*? After all, she had done the ritual at Marie Laveau's grave. She had enough experience to know that when it came to magic, things didn't always happen right away, or in the way you expected them to, but she was getting slightly impatient. They had to report back on Tuesday, and that was only a week away. She had a week to figure out what her most precious possession was.

Well, it can wait a little longer, she thought. It was Mardi Gras, and she was going to enjoy herself. She had a basket of necklaces left and lots of people who wanted them. It was time to get back to work. She reached down and scooped up a handful of the necklaces. Separating out a strand, she flung it into the crowd.

A brown hand shot up and snatched it out of the air. Annie looked and saw the young woman she'd met at the site of Marie Laveau's house standing at the edge of the crowd. She was wearing the same simple white dress that she'd had on before. Annie noticed, too, that she was barefoot. She looked up at Annie with her soft, liquid eyes and smiled, revealing her teeth. She nodded at Annie and slipped the silver beads around her neck. Then, to Annie's surprise, the young woman lifted a hand and crooked a finger at Annie, as if beckoning to her.

Annie was puzzled. What did the girl want? Surely she didn't expect Annie to get off the float. How did she even know it was Annie up there underneath the costume and face paint? Or did she? Maybe it was just a coincidence that the two had come face-to-face again.

The young woman turned and walked back through the crowd. The people seemed to part for her, although none of them looked directly at her, and she moved quickly and easily, without bumping into anyone. Annie watched her go, watched as her head moved through the throngs of people. And suddenly she was overcome with the desire to follow the young woman. She didn't know why, but she knew she wanted more than anything to talk to her.

The float had come to a stop, waiting for the floats ahead of them to turn the corner. Before she knew what she was doing, Annie sat on the edge of the truck bed and lowered herself to the ground.

"Hey," Cooper called out, seeing what she was doing. "What gives?"

"I'll meet you at the end of the route," Annie

called back. "I have to—um—find a bathroom." It was the only excuse she could think of, and she knew it sounded stupid. But she had to follow the girl, and she didn't want Cooper trailing after her.

She turned and moved into the crowd before Cooper could say anything. She was quickly swallowed up by the teeming people, and it immediately became clear to her that she had made a mistake. Standing on the float, she had been able to see where the girl was going. Now that she was on the ground, all she could see was face after face. The young woman was lost to her, and she didn't know where to go.

Still, she pressed ahead, slipping into whatever openings she could find in the crowd. "Excuse me," she said over and over as she tried to get through the wall of flesh that stood between her and the young woman in white.

Finally she came to the back of the crowd, where the people thinned out a little. She was standing on a corner. Behind her was the Mardi Gras parade, while ahead of her were even more people walking in the streets. Voices called out all around her as people tossed beads to people standing on balconies and people on balconies tossed beads back. Several different brass bands were playing all at the same time, and the effect was totally disorienting.

Then she spied someone in white moving very quickly down the street. Annie sped after the figure, not knowing if it was the girl or not but determined to find out. Once again she found herself dodging people and beads. But she was almost there. She could see now that it *was* the young woman she'd met at Marie Laveau's house.

The girl turned a corner ahead of Annie. Annie reached the corner a few seconds later and turned as well. She found herself in an alley, and she stopped. The girl was nowhere to be seen. Besides, Annie had a strong suspicion that being in an alley wasn't the best idea she could have. She decided she must have been mistaken, and that the girl had gone into one of the houses on the street instead. She'd been led on a wild-goose chase, and now she felt foolish. But she could still get back to the float and finish enjoying the parade. She started to turn around.

Then she realized that something was different. Something about the alley was different. She paused. Then she realized what it was—the sounds of Mardi Gras had faded away. In their place was a different sound—the sound of gentle singing. It came from the other end of the alley.

Annie peered down the narrow corridor. The moon overhead shone brightly, more brightly than Annie remembered. It illuminated the alley, turning it into a river of silver. Suddenly it didn't seem dangerous at all to Annie, and she found herself walking down it as though she were walking through a stream.

The singing grew louder as she walked. It was rhythmic, almost like chanting. *It sounds like a circle*, she thought. Then she reached the end of the alley and saw where the singing was coming from.

The alley opened up into a square. On all four sides were houses, their windows filled with burning candles. In the center was a bonfire. It was crackling brightly, and all around it there were people dressed in white, men and women with bare feet singing and dancing. The women swished their skirts, while the men clapped and nodded their heads. And standing near them, looking on, was the young woman Annie had been following.

The girl turned and looked at Annie. Seeing her there, the girl cocked her head and motioned for her to come over. Annie did, going to stand beside the girl.

"What is this?" she asked.

"A celebration," said the young woman.

"For Mardi Gras?" asked Annie.

The girl nodded. "Yes," she said. "For Mardi Gras. But also for other things. The moon is almost full. They have come here to work magic."

Annie watched the dancers. They were circling the flames, putting their hands out over the fire and drawing them back again. She listened to them singing, but she couldn't make out the words.

"What are they saying?" she asked the young woman.

"They are asking Marie Laveau for help," she said. "They are speaking to her in Creole."

"What kind of help?" asked Annie, thinking about the request she herself had made.

The girl smiled. "All kinds," she said. "Some want babies. Some want wives or husbands. Some want to be made well. Some want money." She turned and looked into Annie's eyes. "You asked for help, too, yes? At the cemetery."

So she was there, Annie thought. *I wasn't just imagining things.* "Yes," she told the young woman. "I did."

"And have you received your wish?" she asked in return.

Annie shook her head. "Not yet," she said.

The girl laughed. "I think there is yet still time," she said.

"Not much of it," remarked Annie, sighing.

The young woman pointed to the people gathered around the fire. They were approaching it, dropping things into it. Annie couldn't see what the things were, but she saw their hands moving as they tossed items into the fire and then stood back, watching them burn.

"They are bringing offerings," said the young woman. "Little things, but important things. For some it is simply their wish written on a scrap of paper, for others it is money. Each of them gives what they have."

Annie was familiar with the ritual of giving offerings to the fire, burning something symbolic as a way of releasing energy or giving thanks. She, Cooper, and Kate had done it several times, and it had always made her feel good.

"Will they get what they ask for?" Annie found

herself wondering out loud.

"Perhaps they will," the girl said. "Perhaps they will not. Mam'zelle does not grant foolish requests. Nor will she help those who are not willing to give up something in exchange for what they seek."

Just like my challenge, Annie thought. *They have to give up something, just like I'm supposed to.* But she still didn't know what that something was.

"What do you love most in the world?" the young woman asked her, surprising her.

"My family," Annie answered instantly. "My friends." It's what she had been thinking about all night as she'd ridden on the float, how much she loved having the people in her life who meant something to her.

That's it, she thought. *That's my most precious possession—my family and my friends. The people I love.* She was filled with excitement as she realized that she'd solved the mystery of her challenge. She knew what her most precious possession was.

Almost as quickly she was overcome by sorrow. How was she supposed to give up her family and her friends? How *could* she give them up? That was impossible, in all kinds of ways and for all kinds of reasons.

I must be wrong again, she told herself. *There must be another answer.* But she knew that she wasn't wrong. She *had* figured out the challenge. Only now she was worse off than before, because she knew there was no way she could do what was being asked of her.

Annie turned and looked into the young woman's face. The girl's expression was one of kindness mixed with expectation. "Has Marie answered your request?" she asked.

Annie nodded. "Yes," she said. "But now I wish she hadn't."

"We do not always find what we are looking for," the girl said gently. "But we do always find what we need. Return to your friends now. They will be looking for you."

"Who are you?" Annie asked her. "Why do I keep seeing you?"

"As I said," the young woman replied, "we always find what we need. I am a friend." She leaned over and gave Annie a kiss on the cheek. "Now go."

Annie turned and walked back to the alley. Before entering it she turned once more to look at the dancers. They had resumed singing and were once more circling the fire. The girl was still watching them, nodding her head and smiling. She glanced over at Annie and nodded, as if bidding her farewell.

Annie waved, then walked back down the alley. As she emerged onto the street she was immediately surrounded by the sounds of Mardi Gras. Voices and music filled her ears, louder than ever. It was as if she'd walked through a doorway into a room where the biggest party in the world was going on.

I have to get to the end of the parade route, she thought. *That's where Cooper and Juliet will be waiting.* She wanted to find her sister and her friend. She needed to see them. But what would she do then? How was she ever going to meet her challenge now that she knew what she was supposed to give up? She couldn't. She knew she couldn't.

And that meant she was going to fail.

CHAPTER 11

I feel like I'm twelve again, Kate thought as she stood outside the door to Father Mahoney's office. That's the last time she'd stood there. She'd been taking CCD classes, and she'd gotten into trouble with Sister Agatha for telling Mary Frances Kennedy exactly what a virgin was. When Mary Frances had repeated Kate's information during a discussion about the Holy Mother, Sister Agatha had sent Kate to have a little chat with the priest. Waiting for him to answer the door then, she'd been terrified that Father Mahoney was going to tell her that she had committed a mortal sin and was condemned to spend an eternity in hell, or at least in CCD class with Sister Agatha. But to her surprise, he had laughed when she'd told him what had happened. *Maybe he'll do the same thing now,* she thought as she knocked on the door.

It opened a moment later and Father Mahoney looked out. "Kate," he said. "It's nice to see you. Come in."

"Hi, Father," Kate replied as she entered the office. She wasn't sure what she was supposed to do, so she stood in front of his big wooden desk, her hands clasped in front of her the way they had told them to stand in Sunday school.

"Please," the priest said. "Sit down."

He indicated one of the two big chairs across from his desk. Kate sat down, again putting her hands in her lap. *You have* got *to get over that*, she told herself, and deliberately placed one hand on each of the chair arms. Part of her expected Sister Agatha to pop up from behind the chair and reprimand her, and she had to remind herself that she wasn't a little girl anymore, even if she felt like one.

Father Mahoney sat down and closed a book that had been open on his desk. Kate glanced around his office. It was exactly as she remembered it from her last visit. The tall bookcases were crammed with books. The priest's collection even spilled onto the floor, where books were piled in precarious towers. She wondered if he'd actually read all of them.

"So," Father Mahoney said. "Your father wanted me to speak to you, but he didn't tell me what it was about."

Kate brought her attention back to the priest. He was looking at her with an expectant expression. *He even looks the same*, Kate thought, taking in his silver hair and bright blue eyes. Father Mahoney looked exactly the way Kate thought a priest *should* look.

He was wearing the traditional black suit with white collar, which just added to the overall impression he always gave of having been in the church his whole life. *It's like they grew him at the priest farm and just picked him this morning*, she thought, suppressing a laugh.

She wasn't sure how to begin the conversation. It was going to be awkward no matter how she started it, but she didn't want it to seem like a big deal. *Even though it is*, she reminded herself. *You're about to tell your priest that you want to become a witch.*

"Well," she began tentatively. "You remember that my parents took me to see Dr. Hagen, right?"

Father Mahoney nodded. *Of course he remembers*, Kate thought. *He's the one who recommended her.* Dr. Hagen and Father Mahoney had been friends for many years, although Kate still thought it was a little odd that the priest was so close to someone like her therapist.

"Sylvia and I had dinner just last week," Father Mahoney said. "I take it things with her went well?"

Kate nodded enthusiastically, wanting to make sure the priest knew that he'd made a good suggestion. "Great," she said. "I had a really good time." She paused. "Well, as good a time as you can have in therapy." She blushed, feeling stupid.

Father Mahoney laughed. "You're allowed to have a good time," he said. "Even in therapy. I'm glad you liked Dr. Hagen. She's a great doctor, and a great person. And I know she really liked you."

Hearing that made Kate feel good. She'd shared

a lot about herself with the therapist, and hearing that Dr. Hagen liked her made her feel like she'd done something right.

"I don't know if you remember *why* my parents wanted me to go to therapy," Kate said, deciding it was time to get to the heart of the conversation. "It was because they were worried about my interest in Wicca."

She couldn't imagine that the priest *didn't* remember. After all, her parents had made her talk to him then, too, although then Kate had mostly sat and listened while her parents practically begged Father Mahoney to make her stop going to the weekly study class. All of them had been surprised when he'd suggested therapy.

"I remember," he said neutrally.

Kate sighed. He wasn't giving her any indications as to what he thought about the whole situation, although at their earlier meeting he had asked her all kinds of questions about exactly what she and her friends did when they performed rituals. She recalled, with some embarrassment, asking him in her most sarcastic tone if he was planning on writing a textbook on the subject or something. *Goddess, were you hostile*, she berated herself.

Well, she wasn't feeling hostile now. Just nervous. The priest was waiting patiently for her to continue. "I'm still going to class," she said quickly, determined to get it out. "To the Wicca study class. Dr. Hagen thought it was a good idea," she added, as if somehow this might make the priest think it was okay.

Father Mahoney leaned back in his chair but didn't say anything. *Wow, he's good,* thought Kate. *He should be one of those police interrogators or something.*

"Anyway, the class is almost over. The year and a day. That's how long we promised to study Wicca for. It's traditional."

She was babbling, but she couldn't stop. It was as if her mouth had opened on its own and the words were pouring out.

"So now it's time to decide if we want to be initiated. Into Wicca. I guess it's sort of like when you get confirmed, but different. I mean, you don't have the whole Communion thing, right? Although we have cakes and wine. Oh, but it isn't really wine," she added hastily. "It's usually fruit juice or cider. And I guess it *is* a lot like confirmation because you're dedicating yourself to Wicca for more or less the rest of your life and it's a big deal. And that's what's going on, and my dad said I had to talk to you before I make up my mind, only I haven't even figured out my challenge yet so who knows if I'll even be invited to be initiated. Does any of this make sense?"

She looked at the priest, who had listened without speaking during her speech. Now he raised the side of his mouth in his familiar lopsided grin. "Oddly enough, I think I got it," he said.

"Oh, good," said Kate. "Because I'm not sure I did. Could you explain it to me?"

Father Mahoney clasped his hands together on top of his desk. *He must have had Sister Agatha when he was in CCD classes*, Kate thought in passing.

"Well, I think what you just told me is that you've been attending the Wicca study group. Now it's almost over and it's time for you to decide if you want to become a witch. Is that it?"

Kate blinked. "Basically," she said. It sounded so easy when Father Mahoney put it like that. Why had she had such trouble getting it out?

"And your father wants you to talk to me because he still isn't thrilled about the idea of your doing this," continued Father Mahoney.

"Exactly," said Kate.

The priest leaned back again, tenting his fingers beneath his chin and looking up at the ceiling. Kate followed his gaze, but the only thing above them was a light. Kate waited for Father Mahoney to say something.

"What your father wants, of course, is for me to convince you to not do this," he said finally. He looked at Kate with his blue eyes. "What do *you* want?"

Kate cleared her throat. "Well, I don't know," she said. "I mean, I know you're not going to tell me that you think I *should* do it. Are you?" she tried.

Father Mahoney gave her an enigmatic smile. "Right," said Kate. "In that case, I know I want to do it. I mean, there's this whole challenge thing, but that has nothing to do with whether or not I want to be initiated. I *want* to be initiated. I guess I'm just curious what you think about that."

"I'm never happy when someone leaves the church," Father Mahoney said. "That is what you'll be doing—leaving the church."

He paused, letting Kate feel the weight of his words. She ran them over again in her head. *Leaving the church. He makes it sound like I'm quitting the world's most popular rock band or turning my back on a six-million-dollar basketball contract,* she thought.

"No priest would be happy to see someone leave," Father Mahoney continued. "In the past we probably would have given you all kinds of warnings about how you were condemning your immortal soul."

"But you aren't saying that?" Kate asked.

The priest gave a gentle laugh. "Kate, faith isn't about what's right and wrong. I mean, it *is* about what's right and wrong, but that's just a by-product of the real stuff."

"And what's the real stuff?"

"Knowing what the big picture is," Father Mahoney said. He gestured around the room. "Look at all these books," he said. "Every one of them claims to contain truth. You can open any one of them and it will say this is how things are or that's how things are. Some of them will agree with each other, while others couldn't disagree more."

"Then how do you know which one is right?" Kate asked.

"That's the big question, isn't it?" replied the priest. "How do you know what the truth is?"

Kate waited for him to continue. When he didn't, she said impatiently, "Well, how do you know?"

"You don't," Father Mahoney said. "I mean, you can't prove anything for certain, right? Not about religion and spirituality. I can't prove to you that there's a God out there in the same way that I can prove to you that the sun comes up every morning and goes down every night. I can't prove to you that people have souls that go to heaven when they die the way I can prove to you that combining two molecules of hydrogen with one of oxygen will make water. But I believe those things. Why? Because my experience tells me that those things are true."

"Have you ever thought that something else might be true?" asked Kate. She felt it was a rude question to ask the priest, but she couldn't help it.

"I've studied many faiths," Father Mahoney answered. "And I've found beautiful things in many of them, things that I found uplifting and powerful and moving. But this is my faith. This is where I belong. No one can tell you where you belong except for you, and the only way you can decide where your place is is to decide what it is you believe in."

"But that's so hard when, like you said, you can't really prove any of it." She sighed. "Why is it so easy for some people?" she asked. "I mean, how can so many people just believe stuff?"

"Probably because just believing it is easier than

questioning it," said the priest. "I've been in this business a long time," he continued, making Kate laugh. "I've seen a lot of people come and go. I think basically there are two types of people. There are those who want religion to be the one stable thing in their lives. They want to believe that there's a set of rules that never changes, because it makes the rest of their lives easier if they can believe that. And then there are the people who question. They want answers. They want to know the whys and the hows and the whats. They find it difficult to believe something just because someone tells them it's true."

"Do you think one way is better than another?" asked Kate.

Father Mahoney gave her the cryptic smile again. "Would you buy a car if you hadn't checked the brakes?" he asked her. "For years the mass was said in Latin. Most people couldn't even understand it. Why? Because it was believed that people shouldn't think too much about God and their relationship to Him for themselves. That was the job of the priests. The priests talked and people listened. But then some people started to complain about that. Why can't we talk to God ourselves? they asked. Why can't we have the mass in words we can understand? So things changed. And if you ask me, they changed for the better."

"You have to admit, though, it's a lot easier when someone just tells you what to do and where to go," said Kate.

"Easier, maybe," Father Mahoney replied. "But you don't really learn anything that way. It's like teaching rats to touch a particular button if they want food by shocking them when they touch the wrong one. They don't learn anything about the force behind the shock and how it works. All they know is it hurts if they do the 'wrong' thing."

"So how do I know if I'm doing the right thing?" Kate asked him. "How do I know for sure what's true for me?"

"That's a question only you can answer," Father Mahoney replied. "If it has an answer at all."

Thanks a lot, Kate wanted to say. *Thanks so much for not helping at all.* Then a thought struck her: *That's a question only you can answer. If it has an answer at all.* A question with no answer. Just like her challenge. Was it possible that Father Mahoney had just provided her with the key to figuring out her challenge?

Kate gave a little laugh, this time out loud. What would her father think if she told him that the man he'd sent her to to change her mind had instead provided her with the information to perhaps meet the challenge that would make her a witch? It was too weird.

"Is something funny?" Father Mahoney asked.

"No," Kate said. "I mean sort of. It's not important."

Father Mahoney turned to one of his bookshelves and took down a book, which he handed to Kate. "This might interest you," he said.

Kate looked at the book. It was called *The Seven Storey Mountain*, written by a man named Thomas Merton.

"Thomas Merton was a young man who was on a quest for faith," Father Mahoney said. "His quest led him to join a Trappist monastery. I'm not suggesting that for *you*, but I think you might relate to his story."

"This isn't some kind of trick, is it?" Kate said. "You're not trying to get me all hyped up about becoming a nun or something, right? Because that is so not happening."

"No," Father Mahoney said. "Priest's honor." He gave Kate an innocent look. "Would I lie?" he asked.

Kate rolled her eyes. She was feeling more and more at ease with the priest. But he still hadn't really answered the question she'd come to him with. Or, rather, that her father had sent her to him with.

"You don't think there's anything *bad* about me wanting to become a witch, do you?" she said, finally getting it out.

"You know the church's opinion about witchcraft," Father Mahoney said. "We haven't exactly been accepting and embracing of it over the years."

"No kidding," Kate remarked, thinking about the Inquisition and the hundreds of thousands of people tortured and killed for supposedly being witches.

"I think God comes in many forms," Father Mahoney said carefully. "And I don't think we all find God in the same form. Do you remember the part of the catechism where we ask 'Why did God make me?'"

Kate nodded. They had learned the answer in CCD class. After being reminded of the answer over and over by Sister Agatha, Kate had been able to reply to the question on cue. She did so now. "God made me to know him, to love him, and to serve him in this world and to be happy with him forever in the next," she said without thinking.

Father Mahoney smiled. "Thank you, Sister Agatha," he said, laughing. "Yes, that's the traditional answer. And I think it's a good one. I don't think there's anything greater we can do than to know God as deeply as possible and have our lives be a reflection of that knowing. I like to think I'm sure about being happy with Him forever in the next world as well, but I don't think I'll really find out until I'm there, which hopefully won't be for a while yet."

Kate wanted him to go further, to put everything that he'd said together and say that the Goddess was just another form of God and that it was okay with him if she wanted to dedicate her life to finding out everything she could about the Goddess. But he didn't. Instead he said, "Kate, I want for you what I want for all my parishioners, and really for everyone in the world. I want you to ask questions. I want you to struggle with the answers. And I want you to come away from that struggle a stronger person whose life has been changed by the experience. I'm not going to tell you where to look for answers or what questions to ask. You have to do that. But I will tell you that you will always be welcome here, and my door will always be open to you if you want to talk."

Kate smiled. "Thanks," she said. She still didn't have the answer to her big question, which was whether or not becoming a witch was really the way to go for her. But it was a step in the right direction.

She stood up to go. Father Mahoney stood as well, walking Kate to the door. There he paused. "Tell your parents I said hello," he said. "And tell your father if he has anything he wants to talk to me about, he can come see me."

Kate knew what the priest was getting at. Her dad was going to be unhappy that Father Mahoney hadn't given her a lecture and convinced her to give up any thoughts of initiation. He'd probably want an explanation.

"I'll tell him," she said. "But you might want to think about sending him to talk to Sister Agatha instead. *She'd* be able to handle him."

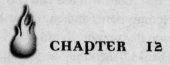

CHAPTER 12

Cooper stood at the side of the stage, looking out at the actors and wondering what in the world she was doing. *I can't believe I let Andre talk me into this*, she thought, not for the first time in the past twelve hours. She looked down at her costume. Juliet and Darcy had done their best to alter it, but it was still a little big, and Cooper worried that she might trip over the hem of the dress. She hadn't been in a dress in a *long* time as it was. Adding the pressure of having to walk, speak, and *act* to the situation made it even more stressful.

It had all started that morning, when Cooper had entered the kitchen, badly needing some coffee after her late night the evening before. After the parade, when she'd finally found Annie (who was being very mysterious about where she'd run off to), Cooper had enjoyed several hours of partying with Juliet, Andre, and some other members of the theater group. They had danced, eaten, and talked until well after midnight, caught up in the Mardi Gras fever. Cooper had eventually fallen asleep on the couch, and had woken up with a sore neck and a wicked headache.

Things hadn't improved when she'd stumbled into the kitchen and found an equally tired-looking Andre and Juliet discussing how they were going to handle a tiny crisis that had arisen. It seemed one of the actors who was supposed to take part in that evening's performance had indulged a little *too* much in the Mardi Gras festivities and as a result was sick as a dog with food poisoning, the result of having eaten a bad oyster. She was currently in the bathroom, retching loudly and frequently, and there was no way she would be able to go on.

As Cooper tried to pour herself some coffee as quietly as possible, Andre and Juliet had discussed their options. It seemed there was no understudy for the role—which was fairly small—and no extra actors available to do the part on such short notice. Andre had been complaining loudly about the impossibility of actors when Juliet, looking at Cooper stirring milk and sugar into her mug of coffee, had said, "Hey, didn't Annie tell me that you do spoken word stuff?"

Cooper, not realizing what she was about to get herself into, had nodded and said that yes, she had done some performance pieces. Juliet had then looked at Andre, nodded at Cooper, and said, "I think we just found you an actor."

The rest was something of a blur. Cooper remembered protesting, as loudly as her headache would allow, but somehow every one of her no's was heard as a yes by Andre. Before she'd really known what was happening, Cooper had found herself running lines with Andre, learning the part of someone called Josephine who was attending a costume party at which a man she was in love with but who was in love with someone else was also in attendance. The play was a comedy, and it was Josephine's duty to provide some laughs by attempting to get in the way of the man she was in love with and the woman *he* was in love with. That's about as much as Cooper got, which was a great deal considering that while she was learning her lines Juliet was simultaneously making her try on Josephine's costume—a very puffy and very heavy ball gown—so that it could be altered. That was the point at which it had become abundantly clear to Cooper that the actor she was replacing was a much larger woman, and that taking over her role meant not only filling her shoes but filling her dress. This had finally been accomplished by padding Cooper's middle with two small pillows, which were strapped around her and secured in the back.

She had been given one opportunity to rehearse her part onstage, with Andre portraying the man Josephine loved and Juliet and Annie taking the roles of the other partygoers. Cooper had managed to remember her lines, and after running through where she was supposed to stand while saying them, her debut with the Night Vision Theater was declared by Andre to be ready for public viewing. Cooper herself was less certain, but nobody seemed particularly interested in her views on the matter, so finally she had just given up.

Now, as she waited for her cue to enter the stage, she was convinced that it had all been a terrible idea, possibly the worst idea anyone had ever had. Yes, she'd performed onstage many times, as a singer with Schroedinger's Cat and the Bitter Pills, and also doing her own spoken word pieces. But this was different. This time she wasn't being herself, Cooper Rivers, she was being someone else, someone named Josephine who apparently was a little too fond of a guy who didn't like her back. Josephine was exactly the sort of person Cooper disliked. She'd already decided that she would *never* be friends with someone like Josephine. However, she had agreed—however reluctantly—to do her best, and that's what she was going to do.

"I wonder who it is behind that peacock mask?"

Cooper heard the line that was her cue to enter. *She* was the one in the peacock mask. Actually, the mask was the best part of the costume. It was made of numerous peacock feathers, all fanning out to form a fan around her face. Her dress was dark blue and purple velvet, so together with the mask the effect was quite striking.

Cooper picked up the edge of her skirt, as Juliet had shown her how to do, and entered. She tried not to think about the audience watching her as she strode as gracefully as possible to the center of the stage, where two other actors were waiting for her. One was the man playing Oliver, her love interest. The other was a woman playing Theodora, the woman Oliver was in love with. Cooper had been instructed to be flirtatious with Oliver while giving Theodora the cold shoulder. It was Oliver who had asked the question about the person in the peacock mask.

"Good evening," Oliver said. "May I ask who has taken up residence behind such a lovely creation?"

Cooper tilted her head a little to the side, trying to appear both dainty and playful. It was her turn to speak. She opened her mouth to say her line, and to her complete and total horror she realized that she had forgotten every single word.

She stood there for a moment, looking out from behind her peacock mask at Oliver, who was wearing a mask made of white feathers, and Theodora, whose mask was made of pink and green feathers, hoping that something would come to her. But it didn't. Try as she might, she couldn't retrieve a single word she'd memorized earlier in the day. It was as if her brain had completely shut down, like a stubborn child sulking in its room and refusing to come down to dinner.

The silence that had fallen over the theater was

awful. No one made a sound. Cooper heard someone cough, and it sounded to her like a thunderstorm. It was as if every tiny sound was amplified a million times, so that someone shifting position in one of the velvet seats could be heard as clearly as if a brass band had suddenly struck up a march.

It was Cooper's worst nightmare. It was *every* performer's worst nightmare. She had had nightmares like this before, dreams where she'd found herself onstage, playing before a sold-out audience, and unable to remember the lyrics to her songs. But it had never happened to her in real life. Now it was happening, and while she wished more than anything that it really was a nightmare—and that she'd wake up from it any moment and find herself safe in bed—it was all too real.

Say something, she ordered herself. *Say* anything.

She took a breath while she searched for words to say. Finally she opened her mouth. "And who might you think it is?" she asked coyly. It wasn't even remotely like her real line, but it was okay.

Oliver looked at her for a moment, clearly confused. But then he seemed to come to life. "Whoever you are, you are most unkind to tease us in such a way."

Good, Cooper thought. That wasn't the right line, either. But she could work with it if she tried. She just had to keep going. *Don't think about the audience*, she told herself. *Just roll with it.*

She laughed as if Oliver had said something incredibly funny. "And who might *you* be?" she asked him. "From your feathers I would take you for a chicken."

The audience howled with laughter. Oliver, who in his white feathers and white outfit did very much resemble a chicken, took a step back. Cooper groaned inwardly. She couldn't believe she had said he looked like a chicken.

"Madam!" Oliver said, pretending to be offended. "You take me for a common fowl? Surely you can see that I am nothing less than a dove."

"And *I* am a hummingbird," said Theodora, suddenly coming to life and joining the conversation.

Cooper stood back, acting as if she'd just seen Theodora for the first time. She had to come up with something to say next. But what? Remembering the reaction the line about the chicken had gotten, she decided to keep going with that. "Hummingbird?" she cooed. "Excuse me if I say that you resemble more a Christmas goose than a hummingbird."

Again the audience howled. This time Cooper felt better about their reaction. The play *was* supposed to be a comedy. Laughter was good, even if it was the result of lines she was making up off the top of her head.

"Me, a goose?" Theodora said. She looked meaningfully at Cooper's distended stomach. "It appears you are the one who has been stuffed."

Cooper shook her head, angrily ruffling her feathers. Now she was enjoying herself. Her original lines were completely forgotten as she launched herself headlong into improvisation. Back and forth she went with Theodora and Oliver, exchanging barbs and trading insults. With each new line the audience laughed more and more. Finally Cooper said to Oliver, "It is a pity that you prefer the mind-less twittering of this silly bird to more refined tastes." She then turned to Theodora and said, "As for you, I would beware. I see several cats among the guests here. If you are not careful you might find yourself becoming someone's dinner. And now good night."

With that she turned and flounced offstage. As soon as she was beyond the curtains she saw Andre standing in the wings. He had a peculiar expression on his face, and immediately Cooper wished she could just disappear. She removed her peacock mask.

"I'm *really* sorry," she said. "I just totally froze out there. I don't know what happened. It was like all my lines just—"

"Relax," Andre said, grinning. "You were fab-ulous."

"I was?" said Cooper doubtfully. "But I didn't say one line the way it was written."

Andre shook his head. "No," he told her. "You

said them better. Cooper, that was *hysterical*. This is supposed to be a classic farce, and you made it even more ridiculous than it was. That line about Theodora looking like a Christmas goose was a riot."

"Really?" said Cooper. She still wasn't convinced that Andre wasn't angry at her.

"Really," Andre said. "In fact, I want you to go write down what you said. I'm going to leave it in the show."

Cooper was taken aback for a moment. "Um, okay," she said, shaking her head as if to clear it. "I don't know if I can remember all of it, but I'll try."

"Go on," Andre said. "Go back to the dressing room and write. I don't want to lose a word of what happened out there."

Cooper ran off to the dressing room, still in shock. She didn't even take off her costume before sitting down at the makeup table and writing down what she could remember of her lines on a scrap of paper.

She had most of it done when the actress playing Theodora came in for her costume change. When Cooper saw her, her doubts returned. "I'm sorry about what happened out there," she said as Theodora removed her wig and mask.

"What?" Theodora said. "Are you nuts? That was a blast. Everyone loved it. You have great instincts. Here, can you unzip me?"

Cooper helped her out of her dress. "I was

afraid you'd be angry," she told Theodora. "I would be if someone forgot their lines."

"That's why this is called acting," Theodora said as she slipped on her next costume. "You have to be able to react to *anything*. That's what you did. You're a natural."

She ran out of the dressing room, leaving Cooper alone. Once again Cooper was overcome with a sense of relief. Mixed with that was a growing sense of pride. She had handled herself really well out there, she thought. She hadn't caved in under the pressure, and she hadn't fallen to pieces just because she'd forgotten her lines.

Another woman came into the dressing room to prepare for an upcoming scene. She smiled at Cooper as she sat down and began to apply some makeup. "You were great out there," she said. "I know I would just die if I forgot my lines. It's my worst fear. But you did it."

Cooper nodded in thanks. Something the woman had said was resonating in her mind. *Her worst fear*, she thought. *Her worst fear*. When she thought about it, it made more and more sense. Forgetting her lines in front of an audience was indeed a terrible fear for Cooper. She hadn't really thought about it before because it was such a terrible idea that she preferred not to even let it enter her head. But now that she'd done it, she realized how true it was. She'd faced a great fear. True, she'd done it without even knowing she was doing it, but did that matter? No one had ever said she had to *name* the fear before confronting it.

She sat down again and opened the backpack she'd set beside the makeup table. Inside was the gris-gris that Sunny had made for her. Cooper picked it up and held it in her hand. Had her greatest fear been revealed to her by accident? It sure felt like it. Looking back, she couldn't imagine anything worse than what had just happened to her. But if she'd faced it and come out okay, then that meant that she'd completed her challenge.

Suddenly she was filled with an overwhelming sense of relief and joy. She was done! She had met her challenge! She squeezed the gris-gris in happiness, then let go when she remembered the dried spider inside. Quickly she put the gris-gris back into her pack. *Thanks, Sunny,* she thought. *I couldn't have done it without you.*

She left her costume on until the play was over, standing with Andre in the back and watching happily. When it came time for the cast to make curtain calls, she went out with the rest of the actors. The audience cheered and whistled when she stepped forward, and she bowed, feeling an incredible sense of accomplishment, both for having performed well and for having succeeded in figuring out and overcoming her challenge.

Afterward there was a big party back at Juliet's

house. Many people came up to Cooper and congratulated her on her performance. The woman who had been supposed to play Josephine walked over, tentatively sipping at a glass of ginger ale, and sat down beside her on the couch.

"Thanks for filling in for me," she said, still looking queasy.

"No problem," Cooper replied. "It was fun."

"I think I'll be able to go on tomorrow," the woman said. "I just hope I can pull off those lines as well as you did."

"You'll be fine," Cooper told her. "Just lay off the oysters for a while."

At the mention of oysters the woman turned a greenish color and excused herself. She was replaced on the couch by Annie, who put her arm around Cooper.

"You're a star," she said.

"Please," Cooper said. "I was already a star. Now I'm a star of music *and* the stage."

"Oh, Goddess," said Annie. "There will be no stopping you now."

Cooper laughed. More than anything, she wanted to tell Annie that she had finished her challenge. But they weren't supposed to talk about that, so she didn't. She wondered how her friend was doing on her own challenge. *Maybe she's already done*, she thought. That would be great. Now that her challenge was behind her, Cooper wanted Annie and Kate to finish theirs as well. It would be terrible if one of her friends wasn't with her at initiation. *I wish I could help them*, she thought. But again, that was against the rules. They had to face their challenges on their own, just as she had.

But had she done it alone? *What about Sunny?* she thought suddenly. Was Sunny's help against the rules? She didn't think so. After all, she'd been led to Sunny's restaurant for a reason. She knew that. It had had something to do with magic, and magical help was okay, she was sure of it. *There's always a reason behind everything that happens*, she reminded herself. Sophia had said as much time and again in their discussions of how magic worked.

Cooper shoved her lingering doubts aside. It was time to enjoy herself. On Tuesday she could tell everyone in class about her experience. Then she could get on with the business of initiation. It was so exciting to think about that now that the path to becoming a full-fledged witch was free and clear. Nothing else stood in her way. Her journey was almost at an end.

"Hey, Cooper?" Andre said, coming over to the couch with Juliet. "Can I get your autograph?" He held out a copy of the program from the play for her to sign. "I like to have everyone in the cast sign one of these," he explained. "It's good luck."

"You'd better get it now," Juliet said, pretending

to be very serious. "Pretty soon she'll be too big to work with little people like us."

"Don't worry," Cooper said, signing the program with a flourish. "I'll be sure to mention you when I win my Tony Award."

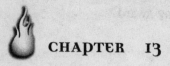

CHAPTER 13

Kate was trying very hard to color within the lines. She had done a good job on the tree, filling in the leaves with various shades of green, but she was having trouble with the cow. She wanted its eyes to be blue, even though she knew cows had brown eyes, but now that they were done they just looked weird.

"It looks like some kind of mutant alien cow thing," she said scornfully, critiquing her handiwork. "Like the cow from Venus."

Still, she was having fun. The crayons had been gift number five from Cooper. Upon opening them on Wednesday, Kate hadn't really understood the point. But when Thursday's gift had turned out to be a coloring book, it had all made sense. Now she was sitting at the kitchen table and filling in pages of the coloring book. From time to time she partook of Cooper's fourth gift, which had been a box filled with assorted candy Kate remembered fondly from her childhood. She'd already made it through the candy corn and the red hots, and now she was sucking on a jawbreaker, determined not to bite it and ruin the fun of taking it out of her mouth from time to time to see what color layer she had reached.

"Playing kindergarten?" her mother asked as she came into the kitchen carrying shopping bags filled with apples.

"I'm taking a break from working on my science project," Kate told her.

"How's that going?" Mrs. Morgan asked as she set the bags on the counter.

"Almost done," Kate told her. She was pleased that she'd managed to get so much done during the week. Not only was the project almost done, but it was *good*. Despite Sherrie, Kate had managed to pull together what she thought was an excellent report. She'd pieced together the transformation of the area around Beecher Falls from wetlands to forest to what it was now. She'd even made a chart linking the rock samples she'd drawn her information from to their respective time periods. The only thing left was to meet with Sherrie one more time to go over everything and explain it to her, so that if Ms. Ableman asked them any questions Sherrie could at least *sound* like she'd done some actual work.

"What are you making?" Kate asked her mother as Mrs. Morgan washed the apples and put them into several large bowls.

"Pies," answered Mrs. Morgan. "Seven of them. I'm catering a luncheon tomorrow and they want pies."

"You sound really thrilled about it," remarked Kate.

"I'm a little pied out right now," her mother said wearily. "Last week it was strawberry pies for a shower. The week before that it was lemon pies for an anniversary party. I just wish people would try something else, like flan. Flan would be nice."

Kate laughed. "I'll give you a hand," she said, shutting the coloring book and putting the crayons back in their box.

She went to the sink, washed her hands, and began to peel apples. Soon pieces of green peel were falling into the sink as she and her mother worked together.

"You haven't told me how your talk with Father Mahoney went," Mrs. Morgan said after a moment.

It was true. Kate hadn't said a word about her meeting with the priest to her parents, mainly because she knew her father was going to be upset. Her mother she was less sure of, but she was still hesitant to bring up the subject.

"It was good," Kate answered neutrally. "He's a nice guy."

Mrs. Morgan smiled. "In other words, he didn't change your mind," she said, saving Kate the trouble of having to say it herself.

"Not really," said Kate.

Mrs. Morgan sighed.

"Was that because you know Dad will be upset, or because *you're* upset?" asked Kate.

"Neither, really," Mrs. Morgan said. "I told your father that talking to Father Mahoney wasn't likely to change your mind."

"But does that *upset* you?" Kate asked again.

Mrs. Morgan picked up another apple and examined it for soft spots. Then she began peeling it. "*Upset* isn't the right word," she said.

"Disappointed?" Kate suggested. "Mad? Worried?"

"None of those," her mother answered. "But thank you for the suggestions. No, it's just that it feels so—dramatic—somehow. I mean, I've learned at least something about Wicca since you told us about taking the class. Plus, Netty keeps talking about it when she calls."

Kate laughed. She knew her aunt was trying to convince her mother to at least *try* something witchy. She was going to a women's retreat in a couple of months, and she was determined to get Kate's mother to go with her. So far Mrs. Morgan had steadfastly refused, but Kate had a feeling she would give in and go. At least she hoped she would.

"But just because I understand what it is doesn't mean I'm totally comfortable with you becoming a—" She stopped, leaving the sentence unfinished.

"A witch," Kate said. "Becoming a witch."

Her mother nodded. "Yes," she said. "That. It just feels strange to say that. My daughter the witch. It's like saying my daughter the elf, or my daughter the unicorn."

"Except that those things aren't real," said Kate. "Witches are."

"I know that," said Mrs. Morgan. "But so many people think that witches are made up. I blame Hansel and Gretel for that, by the way," she added jokingly. "Rotten kids, those two. But the point is, no matter how much I understand that Wicca is a religion, it still feels like it's make-believe."

Kate wasn't sure how to respond. She knew what her mother meant. She knew that many people still didn't understand that witchcraft was real. A lot of them could only think of witches in terms of Halloween caricatures of ugly women with warty noses perched on broomsticks with their black cats on their laps. They had no idea that Wicca was a vibrant religion, a religion with the same legal status as the more commonly known faiths. *Not that legal status has anything to do with making it legitimate*, Kate thought to herself. She didn't need the government to tell her that Wicca was a real faith. She knew it in her heart, where it really mattered.

"Would you be happier if I didn't go through with the initiation?" asked Kate tentatively.

Mrs. Morgan cut an apple in half and began slicing it. "I'd be lying if I said I wouldn't be," she said. "I know it would make things a lot easier for your father, too." She paused before continuing. "Couldn't you just keep going to class?" she asked. "Do you really need to do this initiation thing?"

Kate didn't answer for a moment. She was trying to think of how best to respond to her mother. She wanted to convey how she felt about the initiation without sounding defensive or angry. More than that, she really wanted her mother to understand what initiation meant.

"You know how you went to college," she began, "even though Grandpa Rampling didn't really want you to?"

Mrs. Morgan gave a sharp laugh. "He thought it would be better if I just went into the family business," she said. "As if I really wanted to spend my life running a butcher shop. Have you ever smelled fresh pork?" She made a face and shuddered, as if remembering a particularly awful thing.

"And remember how proud he was of you the day you graduated from college with your degree?" continued Kate.

"He cried," Mrs. Morgan said.

"How would you have felt if he'd said you could go to school but not get your degree?" Kate asked.

"What would be the point?" asked her mother. "Why do all that work and not get the payoff?" She looked at her daughter. "Very sneaky," she said. "But this is slightly different."

"No, it isn't," Kate answered. "I've done the work. For almost a year now I've been studying and practicing. Initiation is the graduation. It's what I've been working for—what we've all been working for."

"But it isn't like it *gets* you anything, Kate," said her mother. "A degree is something you can show to people to get you in the door. It proves that you know what you're doing. This initiation isn't like that."

"It does get me something," Kate said in reply. "It makes me a part of something I want to belong to. It means I'm ready to be part of a coven, to be a real witch."

"But look what you're giving up," Mrs. Morgan said. "Everyone in our family has always been Catholic. That's what we are—a Catholic family. Now you're saying you want to be something else."

"It's not that I want to *be* something else, it's that I *am* something else," Kate said. "Being Catholic should mean more than just going to mass every Sunday, or taking communion, or knowing the prayers. It should mean really believing what those things stand for."

"And you don't?" her mother asked. "You don't believe those things?"

Kate concentrated on the apple in her hand. No one had flat out asked her that question before, and she wasn't sure how to answer it.

"Kate, you aren't just giving up mass and communion by becoming a witch," her mother said. "You're giving up a lot more than that."

Kate understood what her mother was implying. She *wasn't* just giving up the things she was used to in her church. She was giving up something that had defined her family for years. All of her relatives were Catholic—had been Catholic for as long as anyone could remember. If she chose to be initiated into Wicca, she would be the first one to step away from that tradition.

"What do you think Grandma Morgan would say about this?" asked her mother.

Kate tried to imagine her father's mother even *listening* to a conversation about witchcraft. Kate loved her grandmother, but she was a stubborn old woman who clung to tradition like she was lost at sea and it was the only thing that kept her from going under. She disliked change intensely. Kate's brother, Kyle, had been forbidden to ever let his grandmother know he had a tattoo, for instance. Grandma Morgan had even gotten upset when Kate's father had switched brands of aftershave. She had demanded to know why, as if his choice had something to do with her. Kate knew that if she ever found out that Kate had become a witch, it would probably be the thing that pushed her totally over the edge. *You'd be responsible for sending her to a mental hospital*, thought Kate. *Or worse*.

"She doesn't have to know," Kate said to her mother. "It's not like I'm going to start wearing a pentacle all the time, or doing rituals at the Thanksgiving dinner table."

"All I'm saying is think about what you're turning your back on," said her mother.

"That's just it," said Kate. "I don't think I'm

turning my back on anything. I think I'm just choosing a different way of expressing what I believe."

"Which is what?" her mother inquired.

There it was again, the question about what she believed. Father Mahoney had asked it. Now her mother was asking it. Kate was sure now that it was the question to which her challenge somehow related. But why was it unanswerable? Surely she could put into words what she believed about Wicca, and about the Goddess. Surely she could tell her mother what she believed. But when she tried to think of how to begin, she drew a blank. She could tell her mother how she envisioned the Goddess. That was pretty easy. She could tell her what magic was and wasn't. She could explain how to do a circle, and why they did certain things that they did in witchcraft. She could outline the Law of Three and the Wiccan Rede. But what did all of these things add up to? What did knowing them help her achieve? What was the *point*? That, ultimately, was the question she had to answer. But she couldn't do it.

"I need to think about this," Kate said.

"That's all we're asking, honey," Mrs. Morgan said in response. "If you want to keep doing your circles or whatever they are, that's fine with us. Well, it's not exactly fine with your father, but you know what I mean. But before you do anything else, really think about it."

"Okay," Kate said. She picked up a dish towel and dried her hands. "I have to go meet Sherrie now," she said. "I'll see you later."

She left her mother in the kitchen and went to her room, where she packed her things into her backpack. While stuffing her notebooks and rock samples into the pack, she saw the copy of the book Father Mahoney had loaned her. She tucked that in as well. Then she left the house and headed for the library.

Sherrie was, as expected, not there. Since Kate had pretty much finished their science project, she took the time while she waited for Sherrie to arrive to look at *The Seven Storey Mountain*. She'd tried reading some of it the night before, but it had been very dense, and a little boring. Now she tried again.

For some reason she found it easier to get into the book this time. It was an autobiography, and the author, Thomas Merton, had a very plain way of writing. Kate found it interesting to read about how Merton, as a young man, searched for some kind of meaning in religion. She didn't read the book straight through, but skipped around, reading bits and pieces. She was anxious to see what became of the restless Merton, and had just gotten to the part where he decided to enter a Catholic monastery when Sherrie arrived.

"Hey," Sherrie said, as if Kate were the one who was half an hour late.

Kate shut the book and returned it to her

backpack. She doubted Sherrie would have the first clue who Thomas Merton was, but she didn't want her seeing the book anyway.

"Hey," said Kate.

"What thrilling stuff do we need to look up today?" Sherrie asked sullenly.

"Nothing," Kate said. "It's all done. I'm just finishing writing it up. I thought we should go over it, though, in case Ableman asks you any questions when I turn it in."

Sherrie looked at Kate suspiciously. "It's done?" she said. "How'd that happen so fast?"

Because I did all the work, you moron, Kate thought. But what she said was, "Yep. I made the chart, wrote up the findings, and labeled the rocks."

"What did I do?" asked Sherrie. "Or are you going to pretend you did it all?"

I did do it all, thought Kate. "You did research," she told Sherrie. "I just organized it."

"Oh," Sherrie said, sounding as if she actually believed the lie. "That's right, I did."

For the next forty-five minutes Kate familiarized Sherrie with the results of their project. She went over the chart, showing her where the various rock samples matched up and what kind of geological changes they represented. She even gave Sherrie a list of words related to the project. "You might want to know what these mean," she said.

Sherrie looked at the list, then at all of the work Kate had done. "I don't get it," she said. "Why are you doing all of this? I mean, why are you doing it and letting *me* get a good grade for it? Did you find religion or something?"

Kate laughed, making Sherrie look at her with even deeper suspicion. Sherrie's question was more on the mark than she could possibly know. The fact was, Kate had realized that spending so much of her energy being angry at Sherrie simply wasn't worth it. There were much better things she could be doing with it. *Like figuring out my challenge*, she thought. Letting Sherrie share in the fruits of her work was simply a way of using her energy for positive purposes rather than wasting time with negative feelings. Still, she wasn't about to let Sherrie off that easily.

"How do you know all the work I did is *right?*" she asked, gathering everything up and putting it into her backpack. She stood up, put on her coat, and turned to go. "I'll see you in school on Monday," she said. "We'll hand this in then."

Sherrie just looked at Kate as she walked away. Kate felt like laughing. She knew Sherrie was wondering if Kate was serious or if she was having a joke at her expense. *You'll never know*, Kate thought. *Not until we get our grade, anyway.* And that meant that for at least a few more days, Sherrie would worry about it.

Kate had her own worries. Everything she'd thought she'd been sure of—everything she'd thought she'd wanted when it came to her involvement in Wicca—had been thrown into question. *One big question, actually,* she thought as she left the library. And if she didn't figure out the answer to that question, she knew she wouldn't be ready for initiation. It was time for her to do some hard thinking, and she wasn't sure she was ready for where that was going to take her. But she knew that just as she'd taken the first step down the Wiccan path, it was time for her to take another step—what might be her last step.

CHAPTER 14

"That's the house where they shot a season of *The Real World* for MTV," said Andre as they passed one of the mansions that lined the street they were walking down. "We gave those kids such a hard time."

"You should have," remarked Cooper. "What a bunch of tools. It got so annoying hearing them whine about everything. 'My hair isn't blond enough.' 'Why can't I go out with a frat boy?' 'How come *she* gets all the breaks?'"

"Sounds to me like you watched every episode," Andre teased.

Cooper gave him a withering look. "I only saw it because it was on before *Daria*," she said.

Andre grinned. "Okay," he said, winking at Annie and Juliet. "We believe you. Anyway, one night a couple of us from the theater came down here dressed as clowns. We hid in the bushes outside the front door and scared the juice out of those celebrity wannabes when they came home from one of their scripted 'real-life' adventures. You should have heard them scream."

"Too bad they didn't air *that* footage on the show," said Cooper. "It would have been the only interesting thing they ever did."

"The camera guys were laughing so hard they couldn't even shoot," Andre said, as if remembering a particularly wonderful moment in his life. "What a night that was. We struck a blow for quality television viewing."

"Don't let him fool you," said Juliet. "He watched that show religiously. He also watches *Buffy*, *Popular*, and *Seventh Heaven*."

"*Seventh Heaven*!" Annie and Cooper shrieked in unison.

Andre pretended not to hear them. "Isn't that Anne Rice over there?" he said, pointing to a woman scurrying up the walk to a towering brick mansion whose yard was filled with white flowers.

The girls all laughed at his attempted diversion. Andre resumed the tour, telling them stories about the various houses and their residents. Annie listened for a while, but then she tuned his voice out. She was enjoying their last full day in New Orleans, but as the visit drew to a close the matter of her challenge was weighing on her mind more and more heavily. It was especially troublesome since the events of Tuesday night and her mysterious encounter with the voodoo dancers and the girl in white.

Ever since figuring out that her most precious

possession was her friends and family, Annie had been attempting to understand what her challenge could possibly mean. How was she supposed to give away people? How could she even think about that? It made no sense.

For a while she'd thought that maybe what the challenge meant was that she was supposed to *share* her friends and family with someone. Perhaps, she'd thought, it was a reference to her aunt's impending wedding and the fact that she was going to have to share her family and her friends with Grayson and Becka Dunning. That made sense, sort of. It was a way for her to share the happiness she got from being with Aunt Sarah and Meg—and from her friends and the people she practiced Wicca with. Bringing happiness into someone else's life definitely seemed like a worthy challenge.

The only problem with that theory was that sharing her family and friends with Becka and Grayson was a no-brainer. She'd been looking forward to doing that ever since her aunt and Grayson had shown the first signs of being serious about their relationship. In fact, she couldn't wait to have them move in. Already she was planning stuff that she and Becka could do together, and she knew that her friends were almost equally excited about Becka moving to Beecher Falls. Annie wouldn't have to give up anything, except perhaps her own bathroom, to do that.

So while she did it reluctantly, she'd ultimately

decided that that interpretation of the challenge just wasn't right. It had to mean something else. It was only a challenge if it posed a difficulty. Sharing wasn't a difficulty, at least not much of one, so she had to figure out another meaning to the challenge. Time was running out, and if she didn't figure out what to do, in five days she would have to stand up in class and admit that she'd failed.

"Is he boring you yet?"

Juliet's whispered question pulled Annie out of her thoughts and back to what they were doing. Andre and Cooper were a little ahead of them. Andre was telling Cooper the story of some sensational murder that had occurred in one of the houses.

"They found her head in a *box*," Annie heard him say.

"No, I'm not bored," Annie said to Juliet. "I was just thinking. It's Friday already."

"I know," Juliet said. "This week has gone by really quickly. I've had a great time."

Annie smiled. "So have I," she said.

"Was it what you expected?" Juliet asked her. "Was *I* what you expected?"

"I tried not to expect anything," answered Annie. "So it's all been better than I expected."

It was Juliet's turn to smile. She took Annie's hand and the two of them walked in silence for a minute or two, listening to Andre go on and on about the murder. Annie felt her sister's fingers wrapped around her own. She'd held Meg's hand like that probably thousands of times. Doing that, she'd always felt as if she were somehow protecting Meg, keeping her little sister safe. Now she felt as if Juliet was the one keeping *her* safe. It felt good to have an older sister looking out for her. It was a feeling she'd never really experienced before, and now that she had she never wanted to give it up.

Give it up. Suddenly the words of her challenge slammed into her thoughts like a speeding train. Was Juliet the person the challenge referred to? Was Annie being asked to give up the relationship she'd only just begun? The thought made her sadder than anything else she could think of. But maybe that was it. Maybe she was being asked to give up the precious gift she'd received when she'd found out about Juliet and then actually located her.

She couldn't. For one thing, how was she supposed to do it? Was she supposed to return to Beecher Falls and never see Juliet again? Was she supposed to cut off contact with her? Again, she couldn't believe that she would be asked to do something like that for the sake of her involvement in witchcraft. It just didn't make sense.

Even more important, she knew she wouldn't do it. She wouldn't give up her sister for anything or anyone—even if it meant never being initiated and never being part of a coven. She loved Wicca. She loved participating in circles and rituals. She loved discovering how to use energy more successfully.

She loved the chants and songs. Most of all, she loved the people she'd met because of her participation in Wicca. But she wasn't willing to sacrifice her relationship with Juliet for all of that.

No, she told herself. *It has to be something else.* But as hard as she tried to think of something else, the more convinced she became that Juliet really was at the center of her challenge. Somehow she was the key to solving it, and to either passing it successfully or failing it miserably.

"Hey," Juliet said to her, completely unaware of the turmoil going on inside her little sister's mind. "Why don't we have dinner tonight, just the two of us? I'll take you to my favorite restaurant."

"What about Cooper and Andre?" Annie asked. Although she loved the idea of having a last night in New Orleans alone with Juliet, she didn't want her friend and Juliet's boyfriend to feel left out.

"I'm going to suggest that Andre take Cooper on the haunted riverboat tour," Juliet said. "That should more than make up for missing out on a few hours of our company, don't you think?"

Annie nodded. "Oh, yeah," she said. "Put Cooper together with anything haunted and you pretty much have a happy girl." *Andre had just better hope that none of the ghosts decide to have a chat with Cooper,* she thought to herself.

When they got back to the house, a quick conversation in the kitchen between Juliet and Andre set Juliet's plan in motion. Cooper was more than willing to go on the riverboat tour. "I can have dinner with Annie anytime," Cooper said when asked about going. "But how often do you get the opportunity to see ghosts in hoop skirts?"

Shortly after, Cooper and Andre headed out, promising to meet up with Annie and Juliet later. Annie and Juliet walked to the restaurant, which turned out to be a small place almost totally hidden in a courtyard down a narrow side street and behind a gated wall. After knocking at the gate, they were greeted by a solemn-looking man. Juliet took what looked like a silver coin out of her pocket and handed it to the man, who examined it closely. He then smiled and opened the gate for them to enter.

Inside the courtyard, tables were set up beneath several large trees that grew up between the stones. The branches of the trees were strung with tiny white lights, and the effect was magical. Annie felt as if they had entered some kind of enchanted place as they were led to a table in a quiet corner and sat down. It reminded her of the banquet room from the tale of Beauty and the Beast, where all kinds of marvelous things appeared each night for Beauty to enjoy. The waitpeople, dressed all in white, only added to the effect as they moved around filling glasses and carrying out plates of food that smelled absolutely wonderful.

"Isn't this something?" said Juliet. "It doesn't even have a name."

"It's amazing," Annie said. "How did you find out about it? And what was that thing you gave the man at the gate?"

"That was a token," explained Juliet. "Once you're brought to this place for the first time, you can apply for tokens. If they accept your application, you get six tokens. You have to give up one every time you come here."

"That's so cool," said Annie.

Juliet nodded. "They only give them to people who actually live in New Orleans," she said. "And they're very strict about how you use them. You can't give them away or sell them. If you do, you're not allowed back in. I was brought here by a friend of mine who works for the symphony. I couldn't believe it when he told me how it worked. Then I applied for tokens of my own, and they accepted me."

"It's like your own secret club," said Annie.

Juliet nodded. "And the best part is that it's not snobby at all. It's mainly artists who belong. The owners wanted to create a place that was fun and a little weird, but they didn't want it to turn into a tourist trap or a country club type of thing. This is what they came up with."

"Well, I love it," Annie said. "And I can't wait to taste some of this food."

"The jambalaya is out of this world," Juliet told her as they perused the list of offerings. "Then again, so is the rosemary chicken, the haddock with wine and cheese sauce, and the seafood risotto."

"Let's just get one of everything," Annie suggested, unable to make up her mind. "Plus some of that bread pudding I see under the dessert section."

Juliet smacked her lips. "That bread pudding is the closest thing you'll come to paradise in this world," she said. "Definitely save room for that."

By the time the waitress came to take their order, Annie had settled on the jambalaya. Juliet ordered the chicken, and they asked for some oysters to start with, since Annie had yet to try that particular New Orleans delicacy. As they waited for their food, they sat sipping their drinks and enjoying the beautiful evening.

"I have something for you," Annie said after a minute.

"Something else?" Juliet replied. "You've already given me so many things—the painting, the photo album. What else is there?"

"It's another photo," said Annie. She reached into the bag she'd carried with her and brought out a small wrapped gift. "It's one I left out of the photo album."

She handed the present to Juliet, who quickly unwrapped it. When Juliet saw the photo in the frame, her smile faded and she put her hand to her mouth.

"Is this—?" she asked, not completing the question.

Annie nodded. "That's you and Mom and Dad

right afer you were born. They weren't supposed to take any photos of you, but Aunt Sarah snuck one anyway. I thought you might want it."

Tears slid down Juliet's face as she gazed at the photo. She reached across the table and took Annie's hand, holding it tightly.

"Thank you so much," she said. "I can't tell you what this means to me." She looked at the image again. "They look happy," she said.

"They *were* happy," Annie told her. "They loved you very much." She thought about the journal her mother had kept during her pregnancy, a journal that Annie had found and read. In it, her mother had talked about how she knew that the baby she carried inside of her was meant to have a wonderful life, and how it was her responsibility to provide that baby with a way into the world. Annie knew that while her parents were sad to have to give up Juliet, at the same time they were happy that they could be a part of her life.

"I always wondered," Juliet said. "You know, how they felt about me. I love my adoptive parents. They're wonderful. But there was always this part of me that wanted to know why. Why did my birth parents give me up? What did they think when they saw me that first time and knew they would probably never see me again." She looked at Annie and smiled, the tears on her cheeks making her even more beautiful. "Now I know. And best of all, I have you in my life. It's like having two families."

Annie understood exactly what Juliet meant. In some ways she felt the same way about Kate and Cooper. They were a second family to her. She understood what it felt like for people to love you for who you are. And she understood what it was like to finally connect with something that had been taken from you. She'd felt the same way when she'd been able to speak with her parents' ghosts at Samhain the year before, and she felt the same way whenever she looked at the painting hanging in her bedroom, the painting her mother had done of herself holding Annie. It was an amazing feeling, one that comforted and empowered her, and she hoped Juliet was feeling some of that as she looked at the picture of their parents holding her in the hospital.

Their oysters came, interrupting the moment. Juliet placed the framed photo on the table, where they could see it, and she and Annie each took an oyster. Clicking the shells together in a kind of toast to one another, they tipped the oysters into their mouths and swallowed.

"Those are fantastic," Annie said after she'd downed her oyster. "I am *never* going to forget this place. It's just amazing."

"Well, it will be our secret place," Juliet said. "Whenever you come back, we'll come here."

Come back. Annie heard the words, and they filled her with happiness. Juliet wanted her to come back. Annie wanted to do that more than anything. Then the dark thoughts she'd been having all afternoon cut across her joy like sudden rain, the thoughts about giving up Juliet. She still didn't know what that meant, and it was making her crazy. She *had* to figure it out.

I wish I could talk to her about Wicca, Annie thought. *I wish I could explain what's going on with me. But I don't want her to think I'm crazy. Not until she knows me better.*

That's when it hit her. The whole trip, she'd been avoiding telling Juliet about her interest in Wicca. Several times Juliet had asked how Annie had thought to look up the Northern Star adoption search service that had brought them together. Annie had told her that it had been totally coincidental, not mentioning the fact that it had really been because they'd been studying astrology in their weekly class and that an astrological reading had indicated Juliet's existence. She was afraid that would sound too weird for Juliet, and she didn't want to risk alienating her sister now that they'd found one another. If that meant hiding her involvement in witchcraft for a while, it seemed a small price to pay.

But now she realized that in hiding her interest in Wicca, she'd actually been paying an even bigger price. She'd been hiding a huge part of her life from Juliet, a huge part of who she was as a person. It had seemed like no big deal at first. Now Annie realized that it was a very big deal. She needed to tell Juliet about herself. She needed to talk about Wicca, and about how it had brought them together. And she knew that it might totally freak Juliet out. She'd seen that happen with people. *Look at Kate's parents*, she thought, thinking about how angry the Morgans had been at finding out about Kate's involvement in the Craft. *Look at Cooper's mother, and Brian*, she continued, remembering how the supposedly great guy she'd been dating had dumped her after she'd written an editorial for the school newspaper about being into Wicca. Then there were the guys who had attacked them on the street because Cooper was wearing a pentacle, and the police sergeant who had originally thought they were all nuts when they'd offered to help find a missing girl after having visions of her. All of these people had reacted badly. What if Juliet was one of them?

Annie took another oyster, but she barely tasted it as she ate it. *You have to risk losing her*, she thought with incredible sadness. *You have to risk giving away this relationship with her. That's your challenge*. Her choice was very clear to her. She had to tell Juliet, and she had to risk that in doing so she would indeed be giving up her most precious possession. It didn't seem fair, but in her heart Annie knew that it was. Part of being a witch—a real witch—involved taking risks. It also involved being honest, particularly with the people you were closest to. Annie knew she could never be totally free to practice magic and walk the Wiccan path as long as she had to worry that Juliet would find out about her. She'd seen Kate learn that lesson in a very painful way, and she'd seen Cooper do it as well. But she had always been lucky. Her aunt fully supported her. Apart from Brian, no one in her life had ever turned away from her because she was involved in witchcraft. *And Brian was just some guy*, she thought. *Juliet is your sister.* She knew that if Juliet reacted badly to hearing that her little sister was planning on becoming a witch, it would change everything. Annie would be forced to choose. And the real problem was that at that moment she wasn't sure what she would choose. Wicca meant so much to her life, but now so did Juliet. If being a witch meant not having her sister in her life, would Annie stop practicing Wicca?

There's only one way to find out, Annie thought. It was time to meet her challenge. She looked at Juliet, who had just finished eating another oyster and was wiping her mouth. Her sister had a funny expression on her face, and Annie smiled watching her. She loved Juliet, and she loved being with her. She looked around at the lights in the trees, and at the city beyond the gate of the restaurant. She loved New Orleans as well, and would love to visit the city again. Then she glanced down at the picture of her parents holding Juliet. Was she about to give her sister up, the way they had? Like them, she had to make a decision. If she told Juliet about herself, she might lose her. If she didn't tell her, she would fail her challenge. Neither option was at all comforting, and she didn't want to put herself in the position of having to risk one or the other. But she did have to.

She knew that without any doubt. She had to do it because she owed it to herself to be honest with Juliet, and she had to do it because everything she'd learned in her study of witchcraft told her that being true to herself was of utmost importance.

She thought about the voodoo dancers she'd seen on Mardi Gras. They were giving up their possessions to the fire. Was she about to throw her relationship with Juliet—so new and so precious—into the flames? Was it what she really had to give up in order to be worthy of initiation? She pictured the dark eyes of the girl in white. *Go on*, they seemed to say. *Step up to the fire. Mam'zelle will look after you. After all, you paid your pennies.* Then the girl laughed, a laugh that seemed to take away some of Annie's fears, if not all of them.

She closed her eyes. *Here I go*, she thought. Then she opened them and looked across the table at her sister. "Um, there's something I need to talk to you about," she began.

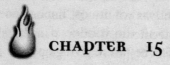

CHAPTER 15

Kate walked down the aisle and took a seat in a pew about halfway back from the front of the sanctuary. It was Friday afternoon. The rain had begun again, and outside the weather was wild. Anyone with any sense was indoors. Kate was glad of this. It meant that she had the place to herself. She had walked through the wind and rain to come to St. Mary's to think, and she wanted to do that in private.

Upon coming in she had stopped at the back of the sanctuary to light a candle. There was a table of candles there, and if people wanted to they could light one and say a prayer or just light a candle to represent the memory of a loved one. Kate had always enjoyed coming in and seeing the rows of candles flickering. To her the burning flames represented the hopes and desires of people who, even though she didn't know who they were, wanted to make some kind of changes in their lives.

She had added her wish to theirs, lighting a candle and asking for guidance in facing the challenge she was hoping to meet there that afternoon. Then she had taken her place in the pew. She sat there now, just being quiet and waiting. Waiting for what, she wasn't sure. But she knew that the sanctuary of the church was where she needed to be, because it represented her challenge to her. Behind her lay the traditions of her past, everything she was familiar with and knew. Ahead of her lay the Wiccan path. Some of what awaited her along that path she was familiar with already, but there was still a lot she didn't know, a lot she was unsure of. If she went forward with initiation, she knew that a lot of the things from her past would in some way be gone. Not everything, but some important things. She would be striking out in a new direction, while her family remained behind.

She knew, too, that this was a challenge her friends were not facing. Neither Annie nor Cooper had been brought up in a particularly religious family. Annie's aunt had encouraged her niece to explore whatever interested her spiritually, and while Cooper's family occasionally went to church, their involvement in it was largely confined to attending services on holidays. Although both Annie and Cooper had faced challenges of their own related to practicing Wicca, Kate was alone in her particular situation.

Her family *was* religious. More than that, they saw religion as making up a significant part of their identity. Now Kate was challenging that identity by being involved in a spiritual tradition they didn't really understand and that they accepted only unwillingly. Her mother had come the farthest in attempting to understand what Kate found so compelling about Wicca, primarily because Kate had unwittingly dragged her family into the world of the Craft when she'd arranged a healing circle for her Aunt Netty. Mrs. Morgan had been extremely resistant to even talking about witchcraft at that point, but in the months since her sister's remarkable recovery from cancer, she had made tentative inquiries about what it was Kate and her friends did. Aunt Netty, who herself had become much more interested in Wicca as a result of her experiences, joked that Kate's mother was like a little kid who was dipping her toe into water she secretly longed to dive headfirst into but who was prevented from doing so by her fear of things lying in wait below the surface.

Kate knew her mother would never become Wiccan. She might be intrigued by it, but she was too attached to her way of seeing the world to let go of it. And that was okay. Something Kate had learned was that there was no one way of believing, no one way of seeing the world and your place in it. The path her mother chose was her path and no one else's, just as Kate's path was hers alone to walk.

But knowing that didn't make her choice any easier. Just because you *could* choose something didn't mean that you *had* to, or even that you *should*.

Whether or not it was okay for her to want to be a witch wasn't the question; the question was whether or not she *should* be one. Was it really the path that was going to take her to the places where she wanted and needed to go?

She looked around the sanctuary. She loved the way St. Mary's looked. It was an old church, made of stone, and Kate had spent numerous Sunday mornings sitting in a pew and trying to count the number of stones that made up the walls and the arches. She never got very far before she couldn't tell one stone from another, so she'd never been able to get anything like an accurate count, but still it was fun.

Her gaze moved over the tall candlesticks that flanked the altar where Father Mahoney blessed the wine and the bread for Communion, and over the large organ situated to one side of the sanctuary. She pictured Mrs. Bingen sitting at it, her hands and feet flying over the keys and the pedals as she played. She imagined the choir singing, filling the sanctuary with their voices.

Then her eyes moved up to the stained-glass windows. Just as she'd often counted the stones in the walls, she had also spent many hours staring at the windows. Each one featured a picture of another saint or religious figure, their faces looking down with curious expressions, as if they were trying to figure out why everyone had come to see them. There was St. Michael the Archangel, with glorious wings sprouting from his back and a spear in his hand. There were the saints Peter and Paul, side by side and all done in shades of green and red.

Before she found out that they were saints and other religious figures, before she knew their real names and their real life stories, Kate had made up stories about the figures in the windows. Her favorite was a window depicting the Virgin Mary. Before realizing that it was *the* Mary, the one the church was named after, Kate had simply called her the Blue Lady because her robes were done in different shades of blue glass. Kate had made up numerous stories about the Blue Lady, and in every one of them the Lady knew exactly what to do to make everything come out all right.

Kate looked at the image of Mary. Because of the rain, her colors were dulled and she looked tired. Yet on her face she still wore the familiar smile Kate had always found comforting. She remembered the first time she had really understood the story of Mary, the mother of Jesus. Thinking about it, she had tried to imagine what it must have been like for Mary, a young girl, to be told by an angel that she was carrying the child of God. *I would have been* so *freaked*, she thought, attempting to put herself in Mary's place. She knew that if some creature ever appeared to her and told her any such thing she would probably run screaming.

Then again, she thought, *if anyone had told me I would be talking to African spirits, helping out dead girls, and preparing to become a witch I would probably have done the same thing.* At least she would have a year ago. But now she had done all those things, was preparing to do the last of them. How had she come to be in the place she was in?

You got here because you believed, a voice in her mind said gently. *You allowed yourself to believe that it was possible.*

Kate hadn't always believed that magic was real or that Wicca was genuine. At the beginning she had thought it was all a lot of nonsense. Interesting nonsense, but nonsense just the same. When her first spell had worked—albeit not in exactly the way she had planned—she had started to change her mind. And as time had gone on and she'd allowed herself to take tiny steps forward along the path, she'd become more and more convinced of the reality of witchcraft. Now she couldn't imagine how she'd ever doubted its existence. Time and again she'd seen the power of Wicca in action.

She herself was the strongest argument for its powers. A year ago she had been primarily concerned with how popular she was or wasn't, and with which guy would ask her to the Valentine's Day dance. She'd been overly worried about her reputation and with how people saw her. Now, after experiencing so many different things—both with her friends and alone—she was someone different. She was stronger and more confident. She knew more about who she *really* was, and about what she was capable of. She'd faced a lot of things and come through changed.

Maybe that's enough, she told herself. *Maybe that's all you really needed to do. Maybe you don't need initiation.* It was a good argument, and a comforting one. But she knew she didn't believe it. Sure, she could stop there and just be happy with what she'd learned. She could never do another magic circle or a spell, at least not as an initiated witch, and she could make her family happy.

But *she* wouldn't be happy. She would be doing exactly what she'd done when she'd allowed her worries about how other people perceived her to affect her decisions. Never again, she knew, would she do that. She was too strong, too determined, to let that happen.

No, the real obstacle facing her was whether or not she believed in Wicca strongly enough to embrace it fully by going through with initiation. Did she really want to declare herself a witch? Did she want to take on the responsibility of publicly choosing to walk the Wiccan path for the rest of her life?

She looked up at Mary again. *How did you know?* she asked the image. *How did you know what you really believed?*

Mary simply looked back at her with the same small smile, not answering. Not that Kate had expected her to. She sighed and leaned back in the pew. How did she know what she believed? In Sunday school they had been taught a lot about what was and was not true. Kate had never questioned it. *Why would I?* she thought. But now she found that questions were all she had. Did she really believe in the Goddess? Did she believe in magic, and in committing herself to discovering the magic within her on a daily basis? How did she know these things were real?

She stretched her leg, and her foot hit the backpack she'd carried with her. Inside it was the book Father Mahoney had loaned to her, as well as the final gift from Cooper's box. The book she had brought to return to the priest. She had finished reading it, and she'd enjoyed it. In particular she'd liked the way Thomas Merton had described feeling restless and confused as a young man. While she could never imagine herself finding the answers to her questions in a monastery, the way Merton had, she understood his desire to connect with something he could believe in.

But how does anyone really believe anything? she asked herself. *There are so many choices. God exists. God doesn't exist. The Goddess exists. The Goddess doesn't exist. It matters. It doesn't matter. There's a heaven and hell. There's no heaven or hell.* Religions were supposed to answer these questions, weren't they? And didn't they, in their own unique ways? Isn't that why so often people with different views on religion came into conflict with one another? Isn't it why she herself was having so much trouble deciding what to do, because she was unsure what she should believe?

She wasn't coming up with any answers. To distract herself she decided to open Cooper's gift. She opened her backpack and took it out, holding it in her hands. It was a box, about five inches square. When she shook it she heard something inside moving around. But she couldn't imagine what it was.

She pulled off the paper and laughed. Inside was a Magic 8 Ball. She'd had one when she was a kid, but hadn't seen one in a while. It was a big plastic ball filled with bluish water, painted to look like the 8 ball from a billiard set. There was a round plastic window set into it, and when it was shaken a triangular die with phrases printed on all its sides appeared in the window, giving an answer to whatever question you asked the Magic 8 Ball. The answers were things like "no," "maybe," "definitely yes," and "ask again." It had been a favorite toy of Kate's, and she thought it was funny that Cooper had thought to give her one.

She looked at the Magic 8 Ball in her hands, thinking. *You might as well*, she told herself. Then, feeling incredibly foolish, she held the toy in her palms and said softly, "Should I become a witch?"

She shook the Magic 8 Ball for a few moments and then held it up. The triangular die appeared in the window, floating up from the ball's murky depths. "Maybe," Kate read. "That's a lot of help."

She decided to try again. This time she asked, "Is the Goddess real?"

Again she shook the Magic 8 Ball, and again when she looked she saw "maybe" staring back at her.

She sighed. "One more time," she said. "Am I making a big mistake?"

This time she shook the ball harder, deciding that she just hadn't been doing it quite right. But when she looked, the familiar "maybe" filled the window.

Kate looked at the Magic 8 Ball in her hands. *What am I doing?* she thought. *Why am I trusting my decision to a stupid toy?* All it was going to say was "maybe." But what if it had answered "no" to any of her questions? Would she have accepted that? And if it had said "definitely yes"? Would she have considered that sufficient justification for making a choice?

The more she thought about it, the more Kate realized that maybe "maybe" was as good as it got. She was never going to have firm answers to anything. All she could do was follow the path that made the most sense to her, that provided her with the things she needed. As for the rest of her questions about what she believed or didn't believe, they could never really be answered. *Like Father Mahoney said*, she thought, *that's why they call it faith.*

She looked up at Mary again. "I guess you just had to take a chance, too, right?" she said.

She put the Magic 8 Ball back into her pack, picked up the book, and stood up. It was time to go. She had come there to find an answer to the question that had no answer, and she might or might not have done it. *If the answer is that there will never be an answer, I'm all set,* she thought as she walked through the sanctuary and headed for Father Mahoney's office to return the book. *And if the answer is that I still don't know if this is the right thing but I'm pretty sure it's not the wrong thing, then I'm good to go.* She had come with doubts and she was leaving with doubts, but she was sure of one thing: She wanted to become a witch.

CHAPTER 16

"I am *so* glad you guys are back."

Kate gave Annie a big hug, then did the same to Cooper. She had just arrived at Annie's house, where the three of them were getting together for a Saturday night sleepover. Annie and Cooper had just returned from New Orleans a few hours before, and it was the first time all three of them had been together in more than a week.

"How did it go without us?" Annie asked. "Did you get lots of work done on your science project?"

"All finished," replied Kate. "And I didn't even kill Sherrie."

"Thank Goddess," remarked Annie. "It would be really hard to explain having that on your school transcript."

"I don't know," Cooper mused. "I hear colleges look very favorably on girls who murder." She winked at Kate. "Did you like your care package?" she asked.

"Oh, it was big fun," Kate said. "Thanks so much."

"What was your favorite thing?" Cooper inquired.

Kate thought for a moment. "The bubbles," she said. Really, it had been the Magic 8 Ball, but she couldn't get into a discussion about that without getting into a discussion about her challenge, and she was trying to avoid doing that. For one thing, she wasn't sure it was allowed. For another, she wasn't sure how Annie and Cooper were progressing on *their* challenges, and she didn't want to look like she was bragging by saying she'd figured hers out. So instead she asked, "How was New Orleans?"

"Fantastic," Annie said instantly.

"Amazing," added Cooper.

"Tell me everything," Kate said. "I want every single detail."

"Upstairs," Annie said, nodding toward her room.

They trooped upstairs and into the bedroom, where Annie shut the door. Cooper took a seat on the floor with her back against the wall, while Kate threw herself onto Annie's bed. Annie sat on the end of the bed.

Cooper and Annie told Kate all about their visit, beginning with the flight there and ending at the moment when she'd walked through the door and greeted them. Kate listened raptly to Annie talk about Juliet and to Cooper talk about the food. As they gave her more and more details, she found herself wishing she'd been there to witness it all firsthand. *But there was a reason for you to be here*, she reminded herself. And she knew she wasn't just trying to make herself feel better. It was true. If she had gone with them, she never would have figured out her challenge. Well, she *might* have, but it was doubtful. Cooper's gift had been a big part of her being able to do that.

"I'm really glad everything went well with Juliet," Kate told Annie.

"I know," Annie said. "It was so hard saying good-bye to her at the airport. But she's going to come for Aunt Sarah's wedding, and that's not too far off. Besides, we took a lot of pictures. I'll show those to you as soon as they're developed."

There was more Annie wanted to say. She wanted to tell them about the strange girl in white, and she especially wanted to tell her friends that she'd told Juliet about being involved in Wicca. But that would mean telling them about her challenge, too, and she knew she wasn't supposed to do that, not until Tuesday's class, anyway. Still, she was just about to burst with the news. She wanted to tell them how Juliet had said, "That is so cool" when Annie had made her announcement, and how Annie had practically cried with relief. It had all been so easy. Well, the ending had been easy. Everything leading up to it had been incredibly hard. While she was telling Juliet about her possible upcoming initiation, she'd been convinced that she was making a huge mistake. She'd been certain that Juliet wouldn't be able to accept that her little sister was going to become a witch, and that she'd lose Juliet the way she'd lost Brian. But that's not the way things happened at all, and Annie was proud of herself for taking the chance, meeting her challenge despite her fears, and in the process becoming even closer to Juliet.

"I can't believe you made up your lines for that play," Kate said to Cooper, allowing Annie to breathe a little easier now that the attention had shifted to someone else.

"I can't either," Cooper replied. "It was kind of unreal."

"How did you even come up with stuff to say?" Kate asked.

Cooper thought about the gris-gris Sunny had made for her. She still had it, tucked into her duffel bag. She hadn't told anyone about it yet. She wasn't sure why, since her challenge was over and it couldn't possibly change anything for her friends to know, but she felt she should keep it her secret.

"I guess I just decided that I couldn't possibly look any stupider than I would have if I'd just stood there," Cooper told Kate. "I don't really remember much about it."

Of course she remembered it. She remembered every single moment of it. It had been her greatest fear, brought to life and put on a stage for everyone in the audience to witness. And she'd overcome it. She'd won. That made her feel really good about herself. *And Tuesday they'll know all about it*, she thought happily.

They sat in silence, looking at one another for a while. All three of them were thinking about their challenges, and how they'd managed to figure them out and meet them head-on. Each one wondered if the other two had succeeded or failed. Finally, Annie cleared her throat.

"I know we're not supposed to discuss our challenges," she said. "But I want to say that I hope you two have learned as much from yours as I have from mine."

Cooper and Kate looked at her. They knew she was telling them—without actually saying anything—that she'd completed hers. Kate grinned. "I definitely learned a lot," she said simply.

"That makes three of us," Cooper told them.

Annie nodded, maintaining her composure. Then she smiled broadly. "In that case, I suggest we do something."

"Such as?" asked Cooper.

"A ritual," said Annie. "A final ritual together before Tuesday. After that we'll all be officially almost-initiated."

"Assuming we all passed our challenges," Cooper added carefully.

"Right," Kate said emphatically. "Assuming we passed."

"Of course," said Annie. "Anyway, assuming we passed, we won't be amateurs anymore, really. I think it would be fun if we did one last one as our little baby selves. You know, for old times' sake."

"Sounds fun," Kate said.

"What do you have in mind?" Cooper asked her.

Annie looked thoughtful. "I think we should do a friendship circle," she said. "Sort of like the first one we ever did. It will be like going back to the beginning again, only this time we'll be celebrating everything we've learned together."

Cooper and Kate nodded in agreement.

"Let's do it," Cooper said.

Annie went to her closet and brought out some candles and incense. She also brought out a cardboard box.

"What's in there?" Kate asked as Annie set the box on the floor.

Annie answered her by opening the box and holding something up. It was a robe made out of bright blue satin.

"Oh, Goddess," Kate said in surprise. "I can't believe you still have that."

"I have all of them," Annie told her, reaching in and pulling out pink and green robes to go with the blue one.

Cooper groaned. "I thought I'd never have to see that again," she said, looking forlornly at the pink robe.

"Come on," Annie said. "You can't tell me these don't hold at least a *few* good memories for you."

Cooper sighed. "Okay," she said. "Maybe they do."

"Good," said Annie. "Then put it on."

She tossed the pink robe to Cooper, who

reluctantly pulled it over her head. Kate put on the blue one, while Annie donned the green. When they were all dressed they looked at one another. Then they started laughing.

"They seemed like a good idea at the time," Kate said when she was able to speak again. She'd made the robes for the Valentine's Day dance that had started her thinking about doing spells, which in turn had brought her, Annie, and Cooper together. Ultimately, the three of them had gone to the dance together, dressed as the three fairy godmothers from the Disney cartoon *Sleeping Beauty*. They had gotten a lot of attention that night, and it had been the first time the three of them had gone out in public together.

"I thought we might want them someday," Annie said. "So I stored them."

Cooper looked down at her pink robe. When Kate had made it, the color matched the pink color that Cooper had recently dyed her hair. Now that her hair was back to its real blondish color, she looked a little silly. Still, she couldn't help grinning.

"Remember the look on Sherrie's face when she saw us in these?" she said.

Kate hooted. "I thought her head was going to explode," she said, recalling the sight. At the time, she had worried that Sherrie would guess that she and her friends were involved in witchcraft. Now she couldn't care less. She'd come a long way in her thinking, and in her attitudes, since that night.

"It seems like such a long time ago," remarked Annie. "Can you believe it's been only a little less than a year?"

Cooper and Kate stopped their giggling and looked more serious.

"So much has happened," said Cooper.

"And it's not over yet," Kate remarked.

"Let's get this circle started," Annie said after they'd stood quietly for a moment.

She began arranging the candles in a circle, and the others helped her. Soon they had their circle. As Cooper lit the candles and Annie burned some incense in the little cauldron they used for such things, Kate went and turned the lights out. Then she returned to the others, and they stood outside the burning circle.

"How shall we cast?" Cooper asked.

"Let's stand at equal points around the circle," suggested Annie. "Then we can go around and each say a direction. We'll just keep going around until we feel like we've raised enough energy."

They spread out around the circle of candles until they were an equal distance apart from one another. Facing inward, they held their hands up.

"Earth," said Annie.

"Air," continued Cooper.

"Fire," Kate called.

"Water," intoned Annie, completing the first circle.

They kept going, with Cooper saying "Earth"

and Kate calling "Air" before returning once more to Annie and "Fire," then Cooper completed the second circle with "Water." The third circle began and ended with Kate, and in this way they kept going around, the beginning and ending point falling to a different girl each time.

The effect of the constantly shifting starting and stopping points was that the energy forming the circle seemed to rise up in a spiral shape, twisting to follow the voices of the three friends. Each of them envisioned it as a kind of tornado of white light, churning with power as it grew stronger and stronger, their voices bringing it to life.

"Earth. Air. Fire. Water." Their voices were continually moving one step ahead of the previous rotation, until it became difficult to tell where they were beginning and ending. First Kate's voice would call to an element, then Annie's, then Cooper's, in an endless chain that circled around and around. They had never cast a circle in this way before, but they found it to be a very simple and powerful means of doing so. When finally Cooper called out "Water" for the last time and Annie didn't begin a new round, they let their voices fall silent.

"Wow," Kate said. "That was like a spiral dance and circle casting all in one."

"That was certainly easier than the first time we cast a circle," remarked Cooper as the three of them stepped into the sacred space.

"Isn't it cool how many ways there are of doing

that?" Annie commented. "Remember how we used to think there was just one?"

They all laughed, remembering how nervous and tentative they'd been when they'd first started casting circles and working magic. Then they'd always been afraid that they were doing something wrong. But they'd learned pretty quickly that as long as their intentions were correct, and as long as they did a few basic things, the rest of their ritual could be done any way they liked. They'd experimented with a lot of different things over the past year, and each time they'd learned something new about working with energy.

Now they seated themselves within the circle. Again, because they had done it so many times now, they could feel the power of the energy they'd raised encircling them, keeping them safe and, more important, providing a space where they could work freely. Sitting in a magic circle always seemed to relax everyone, and it did that now. For several minutes they just sat in silence, enjoying the feeling of being together.

"What should we do?" Kate asked finally, making the others laugh.

"I was just thinking the same thing," admitted Cooper. "We have this great circle going. What shall we use it for?"

"Since it's a friendship circle, I think we should go around the circle and say what each of us values most about friendship," said Annie. "Remember, this could be one of the last times we have our own little circle. Pretty soon we could be working with covens." She paused. "And if we choose to be in different covens, we might not work together much at all again."

A solemn silence descended over them as Annie spoke. It hadn't occurred to any of them that they might wind up members of different covens. If that happened, they really wouldn't work together all that often. They would hold circles with their respective covens, not with each other. It was a thought that made each of the girls realize just what the end of their year and a day of study might mean. It wouldn't be the end of their friendship, but it would be the end of their particular circle.

"Let's make a pact," Kate said suddenly. "No matter what happens, we'll all still be friends. And once a year, whether we're in separate covens, or even in no covens, we'll get together to celebrate everything that brought us together. It will be just us, just our little circle of three." She looked at Cooper and Annie. "Deal?"

Annie and Cooper nodded. "Deal," they said simultaneously.

Kate held out her hands, and Cooper and Annie each took one, joining their other two together. They really were a circle of three, joined in body and in spirit. Each one felt the hands of the others holding hers, linking them together in a chain that had been forged out of friendship and tempered by shared experiences. It was an incredibly strong chain, and each girl knew that no matter what happened, it could never be broken. They'd been through too much for that to happen.

"I'll go first," Annie said. "I'm most thankful that the two of you have become like sisters to me. The hardest thing for me about being involved in Wicca has been dealing with what happened to my parents. The two of you have helped me do that, and that has meant a lot to me. I feel like I've been able to let go of one part of my family because you two are here to be another part of it. You're like a kind of safety net for me, and I wouldn't have done a lot of what I've done if it wasn't for you two."

Cooper and Kate squeezed Annie's hands in response. Then Cooper said, "My turn. I'm most thankful that you two were the first people who really stood up to me and told me what a pain in the butt I can be."

Annie and Kate laughed. "No, it's true," said Cooper. "Before you guys, I wouldn't give people a second chance. Myself included. I thought I knew everything. I thought I didn't need any real friends. But you wouldn't give up on me. First you nagged me until I agreed to join your little foray into witchcraft, then you wouldn't let me drop out when I ran off after that tragic Midsummer. Every time I tried to push you away, you held on tighter. I really appreciate that. It's changed how I see other people, and it's changed how I see myself."

"Well," Kate said after they'd reflected on Cooper's words for a moment. "We're all talking about how we've changed. I know I certainly have. When I did that first spell, I had no idea we'd be sitting here together a year later. I don't think then I could even imagine *talking* to the two of you, let alone being best friends with you. But we are best friends. And what I've learned from you guys is not to take myself so seriously. I've also learned that I'm a lot tougher than I thought I was. Sometimes I can't believe I've made it this far, and I know I would never have done it if you two hadn't been doing this with me. I'd probably still be sitting up in my bedroom with that stupid Ken doll wondering if Scott Coogan really liked me or not."

They all laughed again, thinking about that first misdirected spell of Kate's that had brought them together. It seemed like a lifetime ago, although it had been only a little more than a year since the day Kate had tentatively approached Annie in the cafeteria and asked for her help. Much had happened since then, and they all knew that there was much more in store for them. But for that moment, seated in their circle, they were just three friends holding hands.

"Is anyone else terrified about what might happen on Tuesday?" Annie asked, breaking the silence that followed Kate's speech.

"Maybe just a little," Kate said.

"Oh, don't worry," Cooper told them. "We'll be

fine. Look at everything else we've managed to survive. Do you really think we'd get this far and then not make it?"

She gave the other two severe looks, making them giggle like children being scolded by a teacher.

"You're right," Kate said. "I have total confidence in us."

"Me, too," Annie said. "We'll all be witches yet."

"And when we are," Cooper said, letting go of her friends' hands, "I will *never* wear this robe again."

CHAPTER 17

Tuesday night came much more quickly than any of the three girls had anticipated. When it did, they found themselves sitting once again in the now-familiar back room of Crones' Circle, along with their classmates. There was an air of nervous excitement in the room as people talked more quietly than usual. They knew that since their last class their teachers had been meeting to discuss each of them in detail, evaluating their progress and coming to decisions about their worthiness for initiation. Tonight, after hearing the students talk about their challenges, they would make final decisions about who would be asked to become fully initiated witches and who would not.

"I don't know why I'm so nervous," Annie said to Cooper and Kate as they sat together on the floor. "All we have to do is get up there and talk a little bit."

"Right," Kate said. "A little bit about how we did or did not meet our final challenges—the challenges that can either make or break us. No, I don't see why you're nervous at all." She looked at Annie with a stern expression, staring at her until her friend laughed.

"Okay," said Annie. "I get the point. It *is* something to be nervous about. But we all did what we needed to, right?" She looked at Cooper and Kate, waiting for an answer.

Cooper responded by blowing a bubble with the gum she'd been chewing. When it popped, she peeled it from her face and grinned. "I don't know about you two," she said evilly, "but I know I kicked the Challenge Box's butt."

"Sometimes you're just the slightest bit way too Lara Croft," said Annie in response. "And spit out that gum. You look like a cow."

Cooper gave her a surprised look. "You're not aspecting Freya again, are you?" she asked suspiciously.

"No," Annie said. "I'm aspecting Miss Manners. Now spit."

Cooper deposited her gum in a piece of paper and went to toss it into a wastepaper basket nearby. When she returned, Sophia and Archer entered the room. Instantly a hush fell over the assembled students.

"Welcome back," said Sophia, standing in front of them. She looked around at the faces of the class members, then smiled. "As you all know, tonight is a biggie. We want to hear about your adventures with your challenges." She paused. "And then we're going to let you know whether or not we think you're ready for initiation. That's a lot to do in one night, so let's get started. We're going to go in the same order in which you picked your challenges, which means Kate is first."

Kate stood up and walked to the front of the room, turning to face her classmates. For a moment she almost got choked up looking at them and thinking about how all of them had worked so hard to get where they were. But she composed herself and began speaking.

"My challenge was to answer the question that has no answer," she said, earning some laughs and some groans from the others. "I know," she said, acknowledging their sympathy. "I didn't get it, either. I tried all kinds of things to figure out what this could mean. I thought maybe it was a trick of some kind." She turned to look at Sophia and Archer. "I mean, I know how you guys can be sometimes."

"Thanks a lot!" Archer exclaimed.

"Anyway," Kate continued. "Last week I had to do something I really didn't want to do, something that was in some ways harder even than my challenge. I had to work on a project with someone I don't like. It was this thing with rocks and science and stuff. I won't bore you with it. The point is, in a weird way it got me thinking about the Goddess, and about what I believe about her, and about Wicca in general. Then my father asked me to go talk to our priest," she added, earning more groans and laughs from her friends. "Well, I guess it's his priest now," Kate said thoughtfully. "See, he made me think about what I believe, too. It was like everyone was asking me what I think is true. And what I realized is that you can never really know what's true, not when it comes to things like the Goddess and magic and what we do. You can know what works for you, and what makes you feel like you're learning and growing, but really none of us will ever really know what's true until we die. And maybe not even then," she said.

She looked over at Sophia and Archer, who were watching her. "So I think the question that has no answer is really what is truth, and the answer is that we can never know for certain. I've struggled a lot this year with trying to make Wicca fit into the religion I was raised in, because I was afraid that letting go of that familiar one would somehow be wrong. But now I know that I'm not letting go entirely. Somehow it's all connected, even if I don't really know how yet. And I know that the Wiccan path is the one I have to follow to find the truth—*my* truth. It may not be my family's truth, or my friends' truth, or my priest's truth, but it's mine." She hesitated. "I think that's it," she said, laughing.

She returned to sit with her friends. "That was quite a challenge," Annie said as Kate settled back onto her cushion.

"Way to go," added Cooper.

They listened as the next person went, describing how his challenge had been to create a ritual for celebrating the deity he felt most attuned to, and how he'd accomplished it by building an altar to the Horned God of the forest using items he'd found in the woods. He showed pictures he'd taken of the altar and read the chants and invocations he'd written for the ritual.

"What?" Cooper whispered to her friends. "We could have done that, like, the first *week*. What a lame challenge. Why'd we get stuck with the hard stuff?"

"Everybody got the challenge they needed, remember?" said Annie. "Not everyone is as advanced as you are."

This made them all giggle a little, and they had to try very hard not to disrupt the proceedings. Thankfully, Annie was next to go, and the nervousness she felt about doing her presentation helped them all calm down.

"My challenge was to give away my most precious possession," she said. "I know that sounds like an obvious one, but it wasn't. I really don't think giving someone my bike or my favorite necklace or whatever would really prove anything to anyone. Although that would have been a lot easier than what I *did* do," she added.

She held up a photo she'd been carrying. It showed her and Juliet standing together in front of the Café Du Monde. Cooper had taken it for them, and Annie loved it because she and Juliet had their arms around one another and were smiling as if they were about to burst from happiness.

"This is me and my sister," Annie said. "My big sister, Juliet. I just found out about her, and just met her for the first time last week. I *really* wanted her to like me, and I was afraid that if I told her that I was studying Wicca that she might not. I've had some negative experiences with people freaking out about that, and I know some of you have, too. So I wasn't going to say anything. But then I realized that Juliet was my most precious possession, and I was trying to keep her safe by not telling her the truth about me. I was trying to keep us *both* safe."

She paused, collecting her thoughts. "But Wicca isn't safe," she continued. "I don't mean that it's dangerous, but it can be hard. And it should be hard. That's how we change and grow, right? By doing things that make us think and learn. So if I kept my interest in the Craft from Juliet, I wasn't being safe, I was being dishonest and afraid. If I didn't tell her, it would be like everything I did last year, everything I learned about myself, was wasted."

"What did you do?" Sophia asked gently.

"I told her," Annie replied. "I decided that I would risk losing my most precious possession by telling her. And when I did, I realized that she wasn't the only possession I was hanging on to. I was also hanging on to my fear of losing her, the way I lost my parents and other important people in my life," she added.

"For a long time I let that fear hold me back, and little by little I've been letting go of it over this past year. I know I can't not do things because I might lose someone, and I can't always be afraid that the good things in my life are going to be taken away from me. I *have* lost a lot of things, but I've also received some wonderful things," she said, looking at Kate and Cooper. "I've made wonderful friends. I found my sister. I've been part of this class. I've seen and done things I could never have imagined doing. Each of those things helped me get rid of a little bit of fear. But when I told Juliet about wanting to become a witch, I gave away the last of it. So in a way I guess I met my challenge twice," she concluded. She looked at Sophia and Archer. "Does that mean I get bonus points?" she asked.

As the class erupted in laughter, Archer pointed a finger at her. "Sit!" she said, suppressing a smile.

Annie sat, getting hugs from Cooper and Kate.

"That was some challenge," Cooper told her.

"You haven't even heard the whole thing," Annie told her, thinking about Marie Laveau and the young girl in white. She hadn't brought that up in her presentation because, for one thing, she wasn't exactly sure what had happened and how it related to her challenge. More than that, though, her meeting with the girl in white seemed like something very personal, and not something she needed to tell the whole class about. She would tell her friends about it later, now that they were allowed to discuss what had happened to them in working out their challenges, but otherwise she considered it something personal between her and the Goddess.

They listened to a few more of their classmates discuss their challenges before it was Cooper's turn to go. Then she got up and walked confidently to the front.

"My challenge was to face my greatest fear," she said. "That sounds sort of like a Wiccan television reality show," she joked. "Anyway, like a lot of you I couldn't figure it out at first. I mean, I'm not exactly afraid of a lot of things. For a while I thought maybe I wouldn't even be able to do this. But then I met this old woman who made me this charm."

She held up the gris-gris that Sunny had made for her. "She said this would help me figure out what I needed to do," Cooper explained. "I didn't know how it would work, but it did." She then explained about having to unexpectedly take part in the play, and how she'd forgotten her lines. "And that really was my greatest fear," she said, finishing up quickly. "But I faced it and overcame it."

"Do you think the charm the woman made for you helped?" Sophia asked.

Cooper hefted the bag in her hand, thinking about the roots, herbs, and spider inside. "I don't really know," she said. "I know meeting Sunny definitely felt like something magical. And then the thing with the play happened. So I guess they must be connected."

"But you'd never had stage fright before that?" inquired Archer.

"I'd dreamed about it," Cooper told her. "But it had never happened to me. Let me tell you, though, when it did I wanted to *die*."

The others in the class laughed. Cooper looked at Sophia and Archer. "Is that it?" she asked.

"If you're done," answered Sophia.

Cooper returned to her seat, happy that her turn was over. Now she could just sit and listen to everyone else talk. Then it would be time for the *real* fun, finding out who was going to be asked to participate in the initiation ritual the following month. She couldn't wait for that. As she listened to the next person describing her challenge, she tried to imagine what the ceremony might be like.

"That's everyone," Sophia announced when the last person in the group had told his story. "I must say, I'm impressed. You all had very difficult challenges."

"Some of us had harder ones than others," Cooper said under her breath to Kate and Annie.

"And you all did very well in meeting them," continued Sophia. "As you know, I and the other instructors have been evaluating you over the past year. Now that you've completed the final challenge of your dedication period, we're going to offer some of you an invitation to be formally initiated into Wicca." She paused. "But not all of you will be extended that invitation," she said. "This doesn't mean that you've done anything wrong, or that we don't like you. It simply means that we feel you're not ready to make the full-time commitment required for being members of a working coven. If you aren't chosen for initiation, you can, of course, continue to practice Wicca on your own. You can also, if we think it would be beneficial to you, continue to study with the next class of dedicants and perhaps be initiated next year. Whatever happens, though, we want you to know how proud we are of all of you. You each made an enormous commitment last year, and you've each learned a great deal."

"You've also taught *us* a great deal," Archer added, taking over. "So thank you all for that. Whether or not we work with you again as members of one of the covens, we've all enjoyed getting to know you." She looked at Sophia. "And now I think it's time for us to go make some decisions."

"Some of your other teachers are here with us

tonight," Sophia said, indicating the men and women standing at the back of the room, each of whom had taught some aspect of the class during the year. "We're now going to go in the back and talk a little bit. When we come back, we'll give you our decisions."

The teachers filed out, leaving the students alone. Even after the instructors were gone, though, there was very little talking.

"I feel like we're waiting for some blood test results or something," Kate said, thinking of all the times she'd waited with her aunt for similar results during her cancer treatment.

"Or our SAT scores," remarked Annie.

"You guys are too much," Cooper told them. "Did you hear yourselves? You were *stars*. Trust me, when the envelopes are opened, so to speak, our names will definitely be on the winners' list."

It seemed like hours that they sat there, but really it was only about thirty minutes. When Sophia and the others returned, the students all looked at them anxiously. Sophia looked at their tense faces and smiled.

"It's not *that* bad," she said, receiving nervous laughter in response. "Here's what we're going to do. Each of you will go into the back office one at a time. There you will meet someone who will tell you what our decision regarding your initiation is. And once again we'll go in order. So Kate, you're up."

Kate looked at her friends. They each took one of her hands and squeezed. "Good luck," said Annie.

"Knock 'em dead," added Cooper.

Kate got up and walked past Sophia and the others. As she approached the door to the back office, she saw that it was dark inside. Only a single candle illuminated the room. She entered and saw that the desk had been covered with a cloth. Nothing sat on the desk except for the lone candle, and behind the desk sat someone wearing a hooded white robe and a simple white mask. Kate was pretty sure it was Archer sitting there, but she wasn't entirely sure. The figure indicated the chair on the other side of the desk, and Kate sat down.

"Are you ready to learn of our decision?" the person asked, and Kate could tell by the voice that it was indeed her friend Archer. This made her feel better somehow.

"Yes," Kate said. "I'm ready."

Archer handed Kate a candle. "Hold it to the flame," she said, indicating the candle already burning on the desk. "If it lights, you have been chosen for initiation."

Kate held the candle in her hand for a moment. This was it. This was the moment she'd been waiting for. Had she succeeded? She knew she *wanted* to be a witch, but what did her teachers think?

Nervously, she held the end of her candle to the flame of the other one. For a moment nothing happened. Then she saw her candle's wick burst into flame, adding its glow to that of the other candle.

"Congratulations," said Archer. "Now place your candle beside the first one."

Kate set her candle on the table. She was so happy she couldn't speak.

"Your light has now been added to the circle," said Archer. "Return to the others."

Kate stood up. She wanted to hug Archer, but there would be time for that later. Now it was someone else's turn. Kate left the room and went back to the waiting class. When Sophia saw her come in, she motioned for the next person to go.

"Please stand over there," she said to Kate, indicating the side of the room farthest away from the others. "There will be no discussions until everyone has gone."

Kate went and stood by herself. She knew everyone was looking at her, wondering if she'd been chosen. *Can they tell from my face?* she wondered. She knew she must be glowing with excitement. She wanted more than anything to let Annie and Cooper know that she had made it, but she deliberately avoided looking at them.

Several people went into the back room and came back, joining Kate. None of them said a word to one another, but Kate was pretty sure that at least one of them—a girl who had missed several of the class sessions—had not been offered initiation. She seemed upset, and Kate wanted to say something to her, but she didn't.

Then it was Annie's turn. As she walked to the back, she tried not to let any doubts enter her mind. *You've done the best you could*, she reminded herself as she entered the office and sat down across from Archer.

"Are you ready to learn of our decision?" Archer asked her, as she had asked Kate.

"Yes," Annie said simply, receiving the candle Archer offered to her. Like Kate before her, she held the wick of her candle to the flame and watched. When it exploded into light, she let out a cry of relief and joy.

"You may add your light to those of the others chosen before you," Archer said.

As Annie set her candle among the others, she couldn't help but notice that there weren't as many candles as there were people who had entered the room. Who had failed? Was it Kate? She'd tried to read her friend's expression when she'd come back, but Kate had been looking away from her, so she hadn't been able to tell. She prayed that the absent candle didn't belong to her friend.

"Return to the others," Archer said.

Annie nodded and left the room hurriedly. When she joined Kate and the others who had gone before her, she saw Kate looking at her anxiously. *She made it*, Annie thought happily, noticing that Kate was trying way too hard to appear calm and collected. *She made it. We're going to be witches together.* Now they just had to wait for Cooper to go through the motions of lighting her candle and they could all celebrate.

Finally it was Cooper's turn. She walked quickly to the back room, where she sat down and faced Archer. She noticed the collection of candles on the table before her, and guessed—before Archer even asked her if she was ready to hear their decision regarding her initiation—that the candles had something to do with people passing or failing.

"Sure," Cooper said in response to the question. She took the candle that Archer handed her and unhesitatingly plunged it into the flame of the central candle.

It didn't light. She removed her candle from the flame and tried again. She held it there for a long time, sure that it would soon begin to burn. When it didn't, she looked at Archer.

"I'm sorry," Archer said. "We've decided that you are not ready for initiation."

"What?" Cooper said, not believing what she was hearing. "You're kidding, right?"

"Not all are chosen," said Archer. She reached over and gently took the unlit candle from Cooper's hand.

Cooper could only stare at her. "What do you mean I'm not ready?" she asked again. "I passed my challenge."

"It is time for you to return to the others,"

Archer said. "Your questions will be answered later."

Cooper stood up. A mixture of disbelief, anger, and sadness raged through her. "I'm not going back in there," she said. The idea of seeing her friends and telling them that she hadn't been chosen was more than she could bear. She just couldn't do it. She'd failed. But how? How was it possible? What had she done wrong?

She gave Archer one last look, then walked from the room. But instead of joining the others, she headed for the front of the store. She needed to get away from there, away from her friends and from the people who had decided that she wasn't ready to become a witch. She didn't understand what had happened, and she couldn't face anyone. She had to be alone.

As she pushed open the front door she saw Annie and Kate coming after her.

"Cooper!" Annie called out. "Where are you going?"

"Yeah," said Kate. "Wait up."

But Cooper couldn't wait. She left the store and started running. She ran as hard as she could, away from Crones' Circle and away from her friends. She could hear Kate and Annie coming after her, and she doubled her efforts. She ran faster than she ever had before, and when she looked over her shoulder a few minutes later she saw that her friends had given up on catching her.

Still she kept running. She didn't know where she was going or what she was going to do. But running kept her from thinking about what had happened back at the store, kept her from thinking about the candle that wouldn't light.

follow the
circle of three

with book 15: initiation

"I know a lot of you are looking at your upcoming initiation as the end of a long journey," Sophia said to the seven people seated in the back room of Crones' Circle. "You've all worked very hard for the past year, and now the final destination is in sight, right?"

The three men and four women all laughed and nodded.

Sophia smiled. "Well, you're wrong," she said. "This isn't the end; it's the beginning. It's the beginning of a lifetime of learning and exploring and discovering. Why do you think they call your graduation from high school a commencement service? Because it's the beginning of the rest of your life, the start of the journey you were *really* preparing for when you suffered through algebra and gym class."

There was more laughter from the class members in response to Sophia's comment. Annie and

Kate, the only two members of the class still in high school, looked at one another knowingly.

"Your initiation is really a commencement," Sophia continued. "Your year and a day of study taught you a great deal about yourselves—about your abilities and your weaknesses. You've come to know yourselves better, and you've come to understand Wicca better. But you're still just beginning. I was initiated more than twenty-five years ago, and I still don't know all there is to know about Wicca, or about myself." She paused, looking thoughtful, and then added, "I think probably there are some things about myself I *don't* want to know."

Annie listened as Sophia continued her speech. It was the first of four preparatory classes before the initiation ceremony itself. When they'd begun their year and a day, the thought of initiation had been a distant one. Annie hadn't really even allowed herself to think a lot about the actual event itself because it had seemed so far off. But now that it was just about there, four weeks seemed almost too short a time to prepare. Suddenly, Annie could only think about everything she *didn't* know about witchcraft. It was the same feeling she sometimes got before a big test, like she had forgotten to study something really important and would be asked to write an essay about the topic, or she'd learned the wrong list of events or formulas and would have no idea how to work out the problems.

Relax, she told herself. *You made it this far.* She

looked around at the other six people who had been selected for initiation. Of the nearly twenty people who had started the class, the seven of them were all that remained. Several people had dropped out and others had not been offered initiation.

Like Cooper, Annie thought sadly. She still couldn't believe that Cooper had been one of the people whose candle hadn't lit during the choosing ceremony. She still recalled the look of pain, anger, and sadness she'd seen on her friend's face as Cooper had rushed from the store that night. Annie and Kate had gone after her, but Cooper had been determined to get away from them. Kate had wanted to keep chasing her, but Annie had stopped her, knowing that Cooper wasn't angry at them but just wanted to be alone for a while.

Although the three of them had talked briefly about Cooper's failure, Annie and Kate had talked about it extensively in private. Neither of them could figure out what had happened. Annie had even tried to bring the subject up with Archer once, but Archer had kindly but firmly informed Annie that the decision was a private matter between the dedicant and the teachers, and refused to say anything else. Since then the subject had become one that no one mentioned in front of Cooper, although it was always there, waiting for one of them to trip over.

And it's only going to get worse, Annie thought sadly. The fact was, she, Cooper, and Kate were best friends. There was no way Annie and Kate could immerse themselves in Wicca the way they would be doing after initiation and not be able to talk about it around Cooper. That just couldn't happen, which meant one of two things: either Cooper was going to have to deal with not being initiated with them or . . . She couldn't allow herself to think about the other option. But try as she might, she had to. *Or the three of us won't be able to be best friends anymore*, she told herself.

That, however, was a possibility she couldn't even imagine. Not be best friends with Cooper? *Well, you barely knew who she was a year ago*, she argued with herself. That was true. The first time Annie had even spoken to Cooper was after Kate had enlisted Annie's help to correct the effects of a botched spell and the two of them had in turn had to ask Cooper for assistance. Thinking about the moment when she had confronted a reluctant Cooper in one of the school's music rehearsal rooms, Annie couldn't help but smile. She'd been so intimidated by the tough-acting Cooper, with her sarcastic responses and her cool demeanor. It had taken a lot for Annie to stand up to her and break through Cooper's wall of reserve. But she had, and she had quickly come to appreciate Cooper's unique personality. Thinking that maybe she wouldn't be spending as much time with her friend saddened her.

"We won't be discussing any details of the initiation ceremony itself," Sophia said, bringing

Annie's attention back to the subject at hand. "The real purpose of these last four classes is to get you to think about covens. As you all know by now, many—but not all—witches work within covens. You've seen several covens in action, at least during public rituals, and you have some idea of how things differ from coven to coven. Every coven has its own way of doing things, from casting circles to working magic to celebrating the sabbats. It's important that you align yourself with a coven that you think will both be a comfortable place for you to work and also challenge you to grow in your own practice of witchcraft."

Annie snuck a glance at Kate. Did Kate care whether or not they were in the same coven? Was it important to her to continue working with Annie? Annie realized that she was basing her decision, at least in part, on what Kate wanted to do. But was that the right thing? Annie had assumed that with Cooper gone she and Kate would want to stick together. But maybe she'd been wrong. Suddenly the little circle of three that she, Kate, and Cooper had made seemed to be falling apart, and that scared her more than she wanted to admit.